MAY I PLEASE TASTE
YOU, MISTRESS?

SUCH A GOOD FUCKING
BOY FOR ME, PET.

Copyright © [2023] by [Bex Dawn]

All rights reserved.No portion of this book may be reproduced in any form without written permission from the publisher or author, except as permitted by U.S. copyright law.All rights reserved. No part of this publication may be reproduced, stored or transmitted in any form or by any means, electronic, mechanical, photocopying, recording, scanning, or otherwise without written permission from the publisher. It is illegal to copy this book, post it to a website, or distribute it by any other means without permission. This novel is entirely a work of fiction. The names, characters and incidents portrayed in it are the work of the author's imagination. Any resemblance to actual persons, living or dead, events or localities is entirely coincidental.

Bex Dawn asserts the moral right to be identified as the author of this work. Designations used by companies to distinguish their products are often claimed as trademarks. All brand names and product names used in this book and on its cover are trade names, service marks, trademarks and registered trademarks of their respective owners. The publishers and the book are not associated with any product or vendor mentioned in this book. None of the companies referenced within the book have endorsed the book.

Cover Model Photo Credit: Adobe Stock Image

PA Services and Proofing: Bound To Please PA

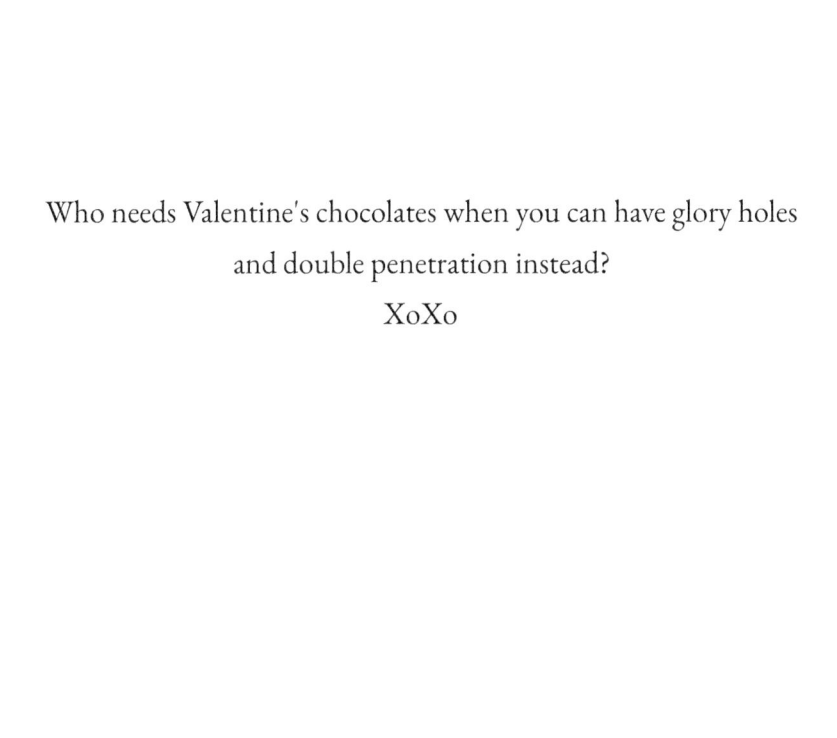

Who needs Valentine's chocolates when you can have glory holes and double penetration instead?

XoXo

POWER STRUGGLE

CARNAL EXPECTATIONS

Bex Dawn

Triggers-Tropes-Kinks

♥ • ♥ • ♥ • ♥ • ♥

-Eating disorder: including but not limited to anorexia/bulimia(not on page) eating triggers, diets, body dysmorphia, family verbal abuse furthering eating disorder, modelling verbal abuse furthering eating disorder, harmful self talk
-MF/MMF (sharing specific in play scene only)
-Dom/Domme
-Dom/Sub/switch
-Femdom/switch
-Submission

-Sex club

-Voyeurism

-Female glory hole (described)

-Male glory hole participation

-St. Andrews Cross

-Edging

-Exhibitionism

-Toys

-Anal play

-Spanking as punishment

-Spanking in play

-Sweetest Aftercare

-Sharing/talk of sharing

-Snowballing

-Fluid play

-Double penetration (toys)

-Degradation

-Praise

-Rough

-Breeding kink/talk

-Filling/Stuffing/Keeping inside

-Choking

-Collaring

-**PET** *swoon*

This novella was written with this song in mind. Enjoy!

Collide by Justine Skye and Tyga

THAT LIST, THOUGH....*WIPES SWEATY brow*

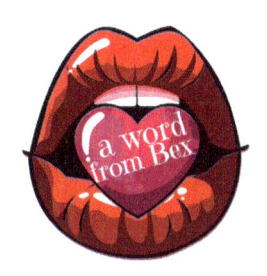

No, seriously. I'm sweating, and I wrote the damn thing!

All jokes aside, on a real note, if you've been with me from the beginning of this series, thank you so fucking much for sticking around as all of these characters have developed. I've loved every single one but I'm not too ashamed to say that even I, the author, have had some faves. (cough, Shiloh and Logan, cough)

That is...until now.

Shi and Logan might have a run for their money with this duo...or quad. Hmm...let's pretend you never read that last bit there. At least not until the end of this book.

So...as a reminder.

This book is about Addison Hughes, Rayvn's co-worker and sometimes friend, and Jackson Lowell, another lawyer at their firm. This book begins four months after he who shall not be named *Noelle Pixie Saint's unfortunate sperm donor* was killed by the great and honorable *bleeeeep*.

If you don't know the answers to all of these teasers, it's because you haven't read Primal Urges or Santa's Baby and I don't want to ruin it for you. They're great. You should pick them up, but I digress. Regardless..this book picks up four months later and if you haven't read those yet, you won't be terribly lost, I promise.

This novella is a sweet, stupidly spicy, basically filthy, non-Valentine's treat.

Grab your vibrators and knots, some extra batteries, some wine, and maybe a cold compress. You're going to need it.

Oh—also make room in your heart for a new book boyfriend. I know I had to.

Enjoy!!

Chapter One

January

Addison

MY COMPUTER PINGS WITH an email alert at the exact moment my desk phone begins to ring. My eyes jolt up from the document I've been scanning for the last ten minutes, and I momentarily debate ignoring both and calling it an early day. The phone clicks to voicemail, and I sink back, relishing the momentary reprieve. My head drops onto the high back of my pink velvet desk chair, and my eyes drift closed.

3, 2—

My phone rings again, and the email notifications on my laptop begin to *ping* in rapid succession. Sighing heavily, I shake myself out of the mental exhaustion that seems never-ending these days and grasp my phone, answering it blindly. I don't need to check the caller ID to know who it is. Only one person's calls are allowed to come through during my workday.

"Yes, Phillip?" I quip, throwing on the confident, badass mask I'm forced to wear whenever I leave my house.

I should stop leaving the house, I idly muse.

"It's an hour past when you typically take your lunch, Ms. Hughes. Would you like me to order your usual?" He's as professional as ever, but after all these years of having Phillip as my assistant, I know better. It's in the slight lilt of his voice. The strain when he asks me about my lunch order. Like he's unsure if today will be the day I go off on him or maybe even fire him altogether. It has me swallowing thickly and rolling my neck uncomfortably on my shoulders.

My eyes flick to the large clock over the cream sofa across from me. Is it only 1:00 pm? Shit. I was hoping it was much later. Clearing my throat, I force myself to smile, hoping the fake joy spreads through the phone and calms his concerns. Doubtful. "I'm not all that hungry today, Phil." I hear a disapproving sound leave his throat, and I quickly amend, "But a salad would be great."

I can practically *feel* him deflate happily through the walls separating our offices. "Sure thing, Ms. Hughes. A grilled chicken Caesar salad, and I'll have them add a vanilla latte for a little afternoon pick-me-up."

This time, my smile is genuine. I don't have many friends...well, any friends these days, but if I did, Phillip would probably be one of them. "Thanks. You're the sweetest." He chuckles awkwardly at the way my voice comes out in a sultry purr.

"No problem," he murmurs. "I'll be back in twen—"

"Phillip?" I interrupt, then immediately chastise myself for being so rude. My heart pounds for some unknown, ridiculous reason. "Make sure that's non-fat and sugar-free." I swallow, my head pounding in time with my heart. God, why am I like this? "Please," I add. *Get it together, Addy.* My lip curls flirtatiously even though I'm alone in my office. *Fake it till you make it.* "And make sure to get yourself something, love. It's on me."

Awkward.

Stupid.

Idiotic.

"Oh, I will. Especially if you're paying," he purrs back, immediately ending my internal spiral. I grin again as we hang up.

That is precisely why Phillip Orion got the job as my assistant over every other applicant all those years ago. He knows me. He knows what buttons he can push and when to cool it. He knows how to handle me at my worst, which, admittedly, is nearly all of the time. My flirty banter and damn near harassing mouth roll off his back without a hitch, and when no one else is around, he gives it right back. We're a great team. If I didn't know any better, I'd say he might be one of the only people on this planet who truly knows *me.*

The idea of him *knowing* me makes me shudder, and I'm suddenly overwhelmed by the thought of what's to come. My mind spins, already planning how we'll make it through the next hour without being obvious.

Sighing, I turn my attention back to my laptop and the chain of emails that have come through in the last few minutes. Flicking through, I find one that has my heart instantly dropping into the pit of my stomach, but like the masochist I am, I read it anyways.

Addison—

Your attendance is required at an event this Saturday night at 7:00 pm sharp. Dress to impress, and for the love of God, do not wear the blue dress you wore in court last week. We saw your photo in the Harold, and it's unbecoming, particularly in the midsection. Have you gained weight? Perhaps you need to increase your cardio. I will speak to Jillian about getting you into a one-on-one Pilates class at the club. As you know, she's likely booked out, but I'm sure your father and I can pull some strings. Lord knows you need it.

See you Saturday. Do not be late, and do not disappoint me again.

Wendi Hughes

My eyes burn, matching the aching lump in my throat, but I quickly blink the tears away. They're useless. I skim over the parting lines again and again. *Wendi Hughes.* No, *'love you,'* or Heaven forbid, *'mom.'* Instead, she signs the brief, shitty email with her full name as though I'm likely to forget the awful woman who gave me life anytime soon. I scoff. I could never, no matter how badly I wish I could.

Shoving up from my desk, I force myself to step away from her hateful words and the thoughts swirling through my head before I can really begin to spiral. Stepping into the bathroom attached to my office, I let the door softly click shut behind me and breathe through the stifling silence created by the cold ceramic and porcelain room. My eyes dart to the shiny white toilet instinctively, and my stomach flips. Exhaling rapidly, I quickly look away and step up to the sink instead, turning the water on cold and submerging my already icy fingers.

I can't remember a time in my life when I wasn't like this. Broken. Messed up. *Wrong*. I stare down at my pale fingers, which are steadily turning pink from the cold, fighting the urge to look up. I already know what I'll see if I look in the mirror, and I already know that I'll hate it.

To the world, I'm Addison Hughes. Also known as *Paddy Wagon Addy*, a nickname that I loathe with every fiber of my being. I'm the top prosecutor in Colorado. My conviction rate is nearly unmatched. I love what I do, and I'm damn good at it. When I walk into the courthouse, I'm noticed and recognized immediately, and it's not just because of my looks. Though, I'm fully aware they contribute to the cause.

I'm tall, slender, and lithe. My waist is tapered. My muscles are toned. My breasts are large and perky, matching my pert ass. My hair is long and blond. My complexion is clear. My eyes are blue. My lips are thick and tantalizingly pink. My cheekbones are high. My jaw is angular and cut. My features are perfectly symmetrical.

And I hate it. All of it. It's not...*right*.

Every single time I look in the mirror, I *cringe*. I hate the person staring back at me. Hate her with a deep, dark passion. I hate her because she is not the woman everyone else sees. The one that a modeling agency recruited at eight years old. The one who was entered into beauty pageants time and time again, winning tiaras until they became crowns, crowns until they became titles. I won money and fame. Was featured in spreads in magazines and walked countless runways. But none of those things was my choice. They came with side effects, repercussions, and harsh judgment that one should never have to endure. If I could go back and take it all away, I would in a heartbeat.

Sighing, I flick the cold water off and swap it for hot, defrosting my chilled fingers as I mentally work through the rest of my day. Things at Attenborough Law have changed significantly in the past few months. Ever since the shit show Rayvn went through last year with Vincent Sutton and Tinsley Snow.

It was no secret that Roy Brandt, our unofficial leader, was opposed to Ray taking such a high-profile case, and he made his opinion on the matter known often and loudly. Sandra Royale, another partner known primarily for being up Roy's ass, agreed with him tenfold for no other reason than to suck up. The rest of the partners, Scott Harrison, Jackson Lowell, and myself, were split, but the three of us agreed that it was Ray's decision and that no one should force her to step down. Unfortunately, the point and argument were moot when Tinsley Snow backed out of the trial only months before Vincent Sutton's untimely death.

Everything should have gone back to normal after that...except—that's not what happened.

A gentle rap on my office door pulls me from my thoughts. I quickly turn the water off, dry my hands and throw my shoulders back as though that one act will clear my head. Unlikely. I step back into my office, calling out for Phillip to come as I tuck myself behind my desk.

Smiling, he breezes through the large room as though it's a runway, his hands full of both of our lunches. "They were quick today," he muses, pursing his lips as he drops the brown takeout bag onto the glass surface before sliding a large, iced coffee in my direction. My lip tips up, and I nod my head in thanks, sliding my laptop to the side to make room for our food. Sighing, Phillip drops into one of the chairs opposite me and rolls his eyes. "We could use the breakroom, you know? Maybe just once. Get to know the new crew."

I cock a brow. "You're welcome to eat wherever you like, and you know it." He scoffs, unwrapping a thick, cheesy sandwich that makes my mouth salivate.

"Like I'd make you eat alone." Swallowing, I shove down the rush of happiness and gratitude that fills me at his words. That is—until he opens his mouth again. "We both know I'm your only friend, and without me, you'd wither up and die an old maid."

I know he's kidding. I can tell by the sassy smirk on his angular face and the wink he throws at me. Still, the words stab me directly in my chest as though they were tossed at me by a mortal enemy rather than my assistant and pseudo-bestie.

Shaking away the unintentional hurt, I grab the clear plastic box housing my salad and peel the lid away. "Whatever," I grumble, stabbing a chunk of lettuce with a plastic fork.

Phillip chuckles around a bite of food, drawing my attention away from my own meal only to find his sandwich nearly gone already. I almost choke on my tongue. *Shit.* Either I'm really behind, or he's really fast. Either way, I need to do something to keep his attention off of me. Clearing my throat, I roll my shoulders back again in a practiced move, forcing my back to straighten and my neck to elongate.

Posture reflects attitude, Addison. If you hunch, you'll have a double chin and belly rolls. Is that what you want? To look fat?

Gritting my teeth, I stab another piece of lettuce with more force than necessary as I imagine stabbing the incessant voice in my head with the shitty cutlery instead. Or maybe its owner. Swallowing, I look back to Phillip, finding him finished with his meal and scrolling on his phone as he sips at his iced mocha, completely oblivious to the way I'm spiraling. "Are you almost done?" he grunts, his eyes flicking toward my salad.

Think, Addy, think.

"So," I purr, blinking rapidly as my full lips tip up. All of his attention turns to my face, and I shovel my salad around in a move that looks absent, but really, I'm digging a hole and making it look like I've eaten more than three bites. In actuality, the thought of eating with such a messy mind has me ready to vomit everywhere. *Think of something to say. Anything.* "What are you doing for Valentine's Day?" I practically blurt.

Phillip leans back in his chair, his lips still wrapped around his straw, and crosses his legs. His head cocks to the side, and his eyes narrow on me. Normally, I'm unaffected by people's stares. At least, on the outside, I appear that way. I've gotten really good at hiding what's constantly simmering just beneath the surface. But right now, with no one else to observe me but Phillip in a quiet, secluded room—I don't feel the need to mask quite so severely. Because of that, I have no doubt that he's noticed how the words *Valentine's* and *Day* make me cringe and shift awkwardly. I hate this holiday with a passion.

"What are *you* doing for Valentine's Day, Addison?" he purrs right back.

Well, fuck. I hadn't thought that through at all, had I?

Fighting a grimace, I primly bite into a tomato, chewing slowly to buy myself time before leaning back in my chair with my drink to mirror his posture. We fall into a silent stare-down—a battle of wills. Normally, I'd win, but right now, I'm slightly rattled by everything tumbling around in my brain and body. The food. The voice that never leaves. The holiday. Thoughts of Attenborough and my old coworkers. Ray. *Him.*

Shaking my head, I exhale heavily. "You know I'm not seeing anyone, Phillip," I finally sigh.

His perfectly manicured dark brows dip down as he squints at me in confusion. He swallows a huge gulp of coffee and points the nearly empty cup at me as though he's brandishing a weapon. "That's not what I asked you."

I tip my shoulder and take a sip of my drink. The bitter, acidic flavor of plain, unsweetened, un-fattened, un-delicious coffee smacks me in the throat, and I barely stifle a gag. Gross.

Better than having acne from the dairy and bloating from the sugar, Addison. My throat tightens at the commentary that sounds almost identically to the woman who gave me life's favorite words.

"If I'm not seeing anyone, then my Valentine's options are limited. Besides," I add, pointing my straw right back at him. "I'd rather just pretend the day doesn't exist at all. It's a holiday created by Hal—"

"Don't," he hisses, leaning forward. "Don't even give me that shitty line sad people tell their friends and family to avoid the fact that they're depressed, horny, and alone on the most romantic day in history."

I roll my eyes and bark out a laugh at that. "Please," I scoff. "Just because a person is single does not mean they're lonely. It means they're strong, independent, and know what they want."

"And what they want is a sad, shriveled-up vagina that hasn't seen a dick since Lucifer knows when and has probably forgotten how it feels to have cum sliding out of you after being well and truly fucked?" he challenges, his eyes twinkling. Meanwhile, my mouth has gone dry. A complete opposite to the situation in my panties at just the mere thought of what he's describing. Well, hell. I do miss that. He's got me there. At my silence, Phillip smirks and turns back to his phone. "Thought so," he murmurs, just as my computer pings with an email.

He gives me a smug look and glances at my laptop without a word of explanation. Huffing, I shove my hardly-touched salad away and turn to my emails. The newest message is a forwarded email from my assistant.

The headline reads: *Be My Naughty Valentine-Brought to you by Kinkster.* Intrigued and confused, I open the email to find a beautiful, discrete invitation for a Valentine's Day party hosted by the Kinkster dating app that both Ray and I had been on months ago. It caters to kink-positive people, seeking like-minded partners in a safe and controlled way. I spent months on the app with no real success, unlike Ray, who scored on the first try. After she met Wolfe and moved away to live with him in New Mexico, I deleted the app, no longer in the mood for online dating. *That's not the only reason; my* annoying brain chides, but I ignore the bitch and keep reading.

Looking to spice up your dating life or enjoy a night of filthy fun with hot singles near you?

Introducing our first annual Kinkster Valentines Bash.

Do chains and whips excite you? How about a glory hole or St. Andrews Cross? Toys? Customized hotel rooms? All of the above?

Join us for a night of cultured debauchery and kinky memories.

Clothing and chocolate are optional.

Flicking through the rest of the flyer, it looks like a party for Kinkster VIPs and their guests to meet with other local singles that are on the app. There's a required background and health check, which I remember being standard from my time on the app, as well as a required form to fill out that goes over your kinks, interests, dislikes, limits, and what you're looking for. It's all standard practice for such a party, from my experience. Much to my excitement, parties like this have been popping up much more frequently in recent years, but this will be the first one I'll be able to attend.

Wait...have I already decided?

A shuffling noise drags my attention from the invitation, and I look up to find Phillip giving me a knowing smirk while gathering up our lunch. "Figured you'd be interested," he murmurs. I swallow, and his smirk drops. Reaching over, he grabs my hand and gives it a quick squeeze that makes my heart pound uncomfortably. "It's time to move on, Addison."

My brows arch in surprise, but he merely rolls his eyes. "Like I'd miss the fact that my badass, man-eating boss had her first real crush." I open my mouth to object, but Phillip shakes his head and steps away. "We don't need to talk about it, Addy. I know that's not who you are, but if you ever want to drop that fortress you pretend to live behind, I'm here." Jutting his chin at the computer as he slowly walks back toward the door, smiling softly. "Until then—fill out the form, meet a sexy man, and get fucked until you're bow-legged and dripping." Winking, he turns on his heel, calling over his shoulder, "I know I will."

Well, fuck. How can I argue with that?

♥ · ♥ · ♥ · ♥ · ♥

Chapter Two

Valentine's Day

Addison

As it turns out, Kinkster's Valentine's Day party is being held at a new posh boutique hotel in downtown Denver called *Omnia*. After filling out the questionnaires, medical documentation, consent forms, and a rather iron-clad non-disclosure agreement, I received a gold leaf and lace invitation via courier. After that, it was just a waiting game.

Unlike what I'd been expecting, there was no line to get in outside. No crowds of excited singles dressed in their sexiest outfits, hoping to score at least once tonight. No signs pointed those of us with invitations in the right direction—nothing but an art deco-style black building with massive, curtained windows.

Men in pristine, black suits scanned the code on my invitation. Once they located my profile on their computer, I was given seven beautiful bracelets, each in a different color. I slipped them on quickly before being ushered inside and guided down a long dark hallway. I won't lie and say my heart hadn't practically been in my throat as I shuffled silently down the long corridor, unaware of what my fate would entail. Stopping abruptly, the suited man opened up a thick, wooden door that almost appeared medieval and ushered me through. I was so nervous that I'm pretty sure I left sweaty handprints down the sides of my black velvet cocktail dress.

At first, I'd been curious as to why a Valentine's Day party required so much paperwork, but after just one minute inside the opulent, dark event room, I understood.

Now, here I stand, glued to the spot, unable to move further into the room as nerves consume me. My breath stutters in my lungs, and my eyes gape as I take in the space. The walls are a deep red and black baroque wallpaper with gold sconces every ten feet, casting a warm glow across the edges of the large room. The floor is dark-stained concrete that's almost unfitting, with the overall luxurious feel surrounding me. There's soft music playing in the background that I can barely make out beneath the low murmur of the attendees as they observe their surroundings. Surprisingly, there aren't as many people here as I assumed there would be. A quick skim tells me that maybe forty or fifty people max were granted an invite.

The waitstaff is mingling about, carrying golden trays with champagne flutes and what appears to be hors d'oeuvres. I'm shocked at their level of professionalism as they do their job, completely ignoring what's happening around them. All the guests I can see are dressed to impress, as the official invitation required. Cocktail dresses, suits, and slacks, all in black, allow our colorful bracelets to stand out.

After filling out all the forms, each approved attendee was matched with other applicants based on similarities. Each match was given an identical bracelet letting us all know, without words, who we'd pair well with. If you see or interact with a match and don't like them, you can remove it and throw away your bracelet. At the night's end, if two (or more) matching bracelets are worn, the pairs can stay and use a customized room. The system sounds more complex than it actually is. In my opinion, it's pretty damn brilliant. I am, however, surprised to find that I matched so well with seven men. I was hoping I'd at least pair with one…but seven? Damn. Your girl has options tonight.

Hopefully, this pans out better than the months I spent on the actual app. Every single date was a flop, and the men were pretty fucking creepy.

My hands skim down my outfit, smoothing the non-existent wrinkles in a nervous gesture. My dress is tight, with a plunging heart-shaped neckline, showing off my curves and chest. I've paired it with black, sheer knee-highs with lace detailing around my thighs that connect to my garters and belt, hidden out of sight. *Who knows. Maybe some lucky guy will actually get to unwrap me tonight and see what I'm hiding.* My heels are black plumps with diamond detailing that matches the thick choker around my throat. My long, blonde hair is up in a high, curled ponytail that accentuates my neck. My makeup is clean and minimal, letting my red lips pop.

Unlike my mother and background would suggest—I didn't find inspiration for my outfit from one of the many high-end catalogs she has sent to my house. No...I modeled my outfit after a similar one in one of my favorite books, *Violet Craves*, where the main character spends a hot night getting railed by three tattooed Gods.

How do you like that, mom? I take my style advice from reverse harem smut books these days, and I'm proud as fuck about it.

I smirk as a shiver works its way down my spine at the memory of how the main female character had been degraded, devoured, and destroyed in the best way all night long. It got even better in the second book when she had a threesome with two of her boyfriends. She pegged one while he sucked the other's cock. I have to fan myself at the thought—hashtag goals.

A particularly loud grunt pulls my attention from my musings, and my eyes trail the expansive room to find its source. It's then that I realize I've been rooted to the spot just a few feet inside the door, too overwhelmed with nerves, excitement, and a heavy dose of shock to move. Shock, because the second I stepped through the door a moment ago, I realized what tonight was really all about.

Sex? Obviously. I'd assumed. Meeting people in the kink community? Clearly. It's stated in the invite. A night of luxury? I gathered it from the gold leaf and lace paper hand-delivered to me last month.

However—what they failed to mention is that this entire party is *interactive* in all shapes and forms.

Swallowing, I hedge forward, deeper into the room. I roll my shoulders back and make sure my neck is held high. With my gut sucked in tight, I allow my 6-inch heels to glide across the shiny floor. Five steps in, and I'm so distracted by the shiver-inducing moans all around me that I run directly into a waiter. Somehow, we steady each other without spilling the tray of champagne he's handing out.

"Sorry," I murmur awkwardly. He tilts his head to the side, looking up a good four inches at my now 5'10 height, and scowls at me. It's so unlike the usual looks I receive from men, especially when I'm dressed like this.

"Watch where you're fucking going, lady," he snaps quietly.

His eyes flick around the room, likely checking to make sure his supervisors didn't overhear him mistreating a guest that paid over a grand to be here. Finding us unsurprisingly alone so near the door when the rest of the festivities are happening further in the room, he turns back to me with a wicked smirk and lets his eyes travel down my body. Clearly finding me wanting, he grimaces. I scoff. Fuck this prick.

It's then that I remember *who* and *where* I am.

I'm Addison Hughes. A woman known for being confident, sexy, and brave, and I'm currently standing in the middle of a goddamned sex party. There is no room for being bashful. My stomach pangs, and my chest thumps as I reach out and gracefully pluck a flute from his tray. I smirk, stepping into his bubble, allowing myself to sink into the one place I truly feel confident: sexual domination.

"Don't worry, love," I purr, leaning in close enough to hear the man, who can't be any older than 23, gulp loudly. "If I'd spilled on you, I'd have made sure to clean you up." He sputters out a cough, making me grin. *This. This is where I ooze confidence. No one can touch this part of me.* I exhale softly, letting my breath fan over his ear. "With my tongue." He sucks in a breath, and I chuckle. "Actually," I coo, trailing a gentle finger over his hand between us. "I think I'd prefer *you* on your knees, licking up the mess you made."

The tray clatters to the ground. Glass shatters, and liquid covers both of our lower halves. Lucky for him, I'm not actually the prissy bitch I pretend to be. I step back just as a much older man in a matching waitstaff outfit appears. His face is red as a tomato as he glowers at the little asshole.

Bingo.

I turn all of my attention to the newcomer, completely dismissing the waiter. I give him a sweet smile tinged with an apology. "I am so, so sorry, Sir. I'm not sure what happened."

He stops in his tracks and does a double-take. His perusal of my body is much more subdued and discrete than the kids. The man swallows thickly and smiles widely. "Are you okay, Miss?" *Miss. Like angels to my ears.* "I can speak to the event coordinator about having—"

I place a comforting hand on his shoulder and give it a squeeze. Before, I'd been putting on a show. Now, I genuinely feel bad for his panic. A quick flick of my eyes at the little prick shows he's now glaring daggers into the side of my head. Yeah—I don't feel bad for him one bit. Looking back at the older gentleman, I squeeze his shoulder once more and step away.

"No worries. I'm totally fine. I appreciate your concern." Smiling at the angry kid, I tip my head. "Hope your night gets better." With that, I turn around, elated when I hear whom I can only assume is the kid's manager going in on him in a sharp whisper.

I'm not too proud to admit there's a new pep in my step as I head back toward the small crowd that's assembled just to my left. Luckily for me, I'm tall for a woman and even taller in my heels. Bringing my glass up to my lips as I reach them, I'm preparing to take a sip when I finally catch sight of what's gotten so many people's attention.

Holy fucking hell.

Apparently, the invitation wasn't kidding when they brought up glory holes. A fact that's proven when my eyes lock on the sight of a curvy woman's naked ass and bare thighs in nothing but a pair of red stilettos. She's bent in half and completely on display for the crowd, as are the two men behind her, stroking their cocks as their rain down handprints on her juicy cheeks. Her upper body is hidden behind the wall, and her pelvis rests on a cushioned pad that lines the small square her body's squeezed into. The red and black wallpaper to the right and left of her is adorned with various high-end sex toys hanging on hooks for her pleasure and whoever chooses to step up and play.

A sharp zap of lust hits me right in the clit, and my knees buckle at the force of it. Just before I further embarrass myself by falling out of pure lust, a strong arm bands around my waist, catching me and keeping me steady. I gasp, more from the tingles that race through my body at the contact than his sudden appearance. I glance down at the stranger's arm, finding a black shirt rolled up at the sleeves, exposing a dusting of blonde hair across his veiny, corded forearm. But what catches my full attention is the color of his bracelet—purple, in the exact same shade as one of my own.

And the fact that he's only wearing one.

We're a match, is the last thought I have before he whispers in my ear, sending shockwaves through my body.

"*Already causing trouble, Addison?*"

Chapter Three

SHE'S HERE. OF COURSE, I knew she'd be here, but actually seeing *her*, here, in the middle of a goddamned sex party, is, well—it's fucking mind-blowing.

Addison Hughes is a 10 in any room. This one is no different. The short black dress clings to every inch of her stunning body in ways that should be illegal. And don't even get me started on the fucking knee-highs. She's trying to kill me, I swear.

Except—she didn't even know you would be here, idiot.

I cringe at the reminder. She didn't know I was going to be here, and given the fact that we haven't spoken since the practice disbanded last November, she'd have no reason to expect my presence. Thank God for our meddling assistants who have remained friends despite the distance between all of us. Phillip, Addy's long-time assistant, called mine, Margie, letting her know that he needed to speak to me immediately. I should have known, judging by Margie's smirk, that something was up. Unfortunately, I'd been too freaked out, assuming the worst. Visions of Addy in the hospital, or worse, filled my brain, and I'd immediately called him back. Come to find out, Phill had set a series of events in motion that would result in Addison attending tonight's events. After a thinly veiled threat to me, my manhood, and my future, I agreed to be a part of his meddling scheme.

I chuckle softly as I remember the way he hissed at me. I believe his exact words were: *"Since you've failed to man up, she's moving on, Jackson. She's going back into the dating world with or without you."* Before ever so ineloquently barking: *"Shit or get off the pot."*

It's not that I hadn't realized so much time had passed. Of course, I did. I was in agony every single day that she was gone. *Even longer, if I'm being honest.* Four miserable months without her perfect, white smile and those dimples that drive me mad. Four months without hearing her sultry voice and shiver-inducing laugh. A laugh that, if I didn't know any better, I'd swear is haunting the recesses of my brain. Her dry humor. Her clumsy mouth that spits out words unintentionally when she gets nervous or upset. Fuck, I even miss the fire in her icy blue eyes when she's pissed off at me.

After going so long without getting my daily Addison fix, seeing her feels equivalent to breathing fresh air after spending months in a shitty porta-potty. Pun absolutely intended.

My eyes rake over her as she leans in and murmurs something unintelligible to the waiter I'd seen shooting longing looks at her from across the room when she first arrived. In an instant, my heart is thumping painfully in my chest. I know Addy. I know the kind of men she usually goes for. I know her power plays and game plans. I've spent enough time with her in bars after work when the team would all get together in the early days. I've seen her pick up men easily and the way they foam at the mouth over her demanding, sexy presence. I've heard her gabbing in the break room at the old office, talking to Phil and Ray about her most recent conquests or adventures on the very dating app that brought us here tonight. Because of that—I also know I'm not her usual type. The younger man holding a tray of drinks, with an attitude I've no doubt she'd love to fuck right out of him...definitely her type.

This right here was my main hang-up in following Phillip's plan. With my connections, it was simple enough to secure an invite to the exclusive event. I knew I'd pass the background and medical evaluations, even though I know I could have had the documents forged, just like my invitation. I also had no doubt that our interests would line up enough to make us natural matches, especially with the modifications I made to my application...*something I'd only do for her.* I knew I'd match with Addison. I made sure of it. The problem is... I'm not the only one who matched with her. A fact that's confirmed by the stack of colored bracelets on her wrist.

What if I have to watch her walk away with someone else tonight? What if she goes upstairs into one of those fancy-ass sex rooms and fucks a man who isn't me? Maybe I should have taken that cocky asshole's advice and fucked with Addy's match results.

My stomach sours at the thought. It's only compounded by the sight of her trailing her sweet, delicate finger across the idiot kid's arm. A growl builds in my throat, and before I know what I'm doing, I step toward them. But then, I see the tray crash to the floor. I watch with rapt attention as she steps back and smirks at the kid, and all my anxiety wooshes away in an instant. I also know Addy well enough to recognize *that* particular look. She isn't trying to hook up or play with him. She's fucking with him and putting the kid in his place.

I continue to observe from my spot on the far side of the room, away from groping hands and flirtatious conversations. I'm not opposed to flirting idly or taking part in the various events happening around the room. I may be a bi-sexual Pleasure Dom, but I'm also a voyeur as well as a rope bunny. My kinks and quirks know very few bounds, and there are absolutely some things going on in this room that have piqued my interest.

However, nothing, and I do mean nothing, is more interesting than my girl and the way she effortlessly brings men to their knees, metaphorically and physically.

Addison turns on her heel and walks away from the waiter and who I can only assume is his manager, and heads toward the first display that caught my eye when I arrived. I smirk, slowly trailing behind her. She pauses on the outskirts of the small crowd around the glory hole. A waitress passes me, holding a collection of shot glasses. She smiles softly and offers it up to me. Unwilling to look away from Addison, I grab the first one my hand connects with a shoot it back. The harsh burn of Bourbon ignites in a slow, fiery path down my throat, but it's quickly quelled by the nervous pit in my stomach. *It's go time.* Without thought, I exchange the empty shot glass for another.

"Oh, Sir, that's vod—" she begins. I shrug and tip it back, uncaring that I've now mixed three types of alcohol in less than thirty minutes. Fuck it. If I'm going down tonight, I'll need the buzz.

Nodding at the poor confused waitress, I drop the glass down and head toward Addy, full steam, without pause. A loud groan followed by the distinct sound of a heavy hand slapping a plush ass fills the space between us seconds before I see my girl's knees wobble. Three long glides, and I have my arm wrapped around her thin waist.

Smaller, my mind barks. *She's smaller than she was before.* My heart feels like there's a tight fist wrapped around it. *Oh, Addy*, I swallow. I thought she'd been doing better. *She was, before you left*, my mind tacks on.

Before I can spiral down that particular rabbit hole, Addison gasps. I notice then that her eyes have dropped down to the lilac bracelet on my wrist that perfectly matches one of hers. My eye twitches at the sight of the others adorning her delicate arm. *Not for long*, I remind myself. Feeling moderately better, I tighten my grip on her with one arm, and drop my hand to her opposite hip, giving it a squeeze. Thinking back to the show she put on just moments ago, I brush my lips across the sensitive skin behind in ear in a way I've wanted to for so fucking long.

Years. I've loved this woman for years.

"Already causing trouble, Addison?" I whisper, using her full name instead of the hundreds of other things I'd love to call her.

Princess. Baby. Good girl. Perfect little slut. Mistress. Wife.

Mine.

Chapter Four

AT FIRST, I THINK she's stopped breathing. My mind tells me to let her go. To walk away. Not to fight her if she tries to leave me standing here. I know she has the right to. But I did that before. I gave her space, knowing how much she struggles with connections and vulnerability. I thought I was letting her process the connection between us. The chemistry. The *feelings*. Instead, she bolted, and like the coward I am, I let her.

No more. I'm here, and I'll be fucked if I let her go again. So, when her brain inevitably restarts, and she finally puts two and two together, I'm prepared.

"What the actual fuck, Jackson?" she hisses. Her body tenses as she tries to pull away. I refuse to let her. My arm tightens around her waist to the point of pain, but still, I hold on. Every inch of her is aligned with every inch of me, and I've never felt anything more right.

I know without a shadow of a doubt that if she'd just let herself—if she'd give in, she'd feel it too. That isn't me being cocky or trying to force something where it doesn't exist… that's the whole truth and the exact reason she ran away before. She got scared. She panicked and reacted the only way she knew how. She lashed out and left me. The mistake she made was not realizing that I'd take her panic. I'd take her anxiety. If she needed to lash out, I'd take that, too. I'd let Addison Hughes walk all over my naked body wearing nothing but her 6-inch stilettos and call me names if that's what it took to prove my feelings and loyalty. A point I'm willing to prove tonight.

"Miss me?" I murmur with a chuckle. Her free hand wraps around the forearm banded over her middle, and she digs her sharp nails into my skin. I huff out a breath and roll my eyes. "Fight me all you want, Kitten. I'm not letting you go again." There. I put it on the table for her. Plain and simple. She can't possibly get my words twisted this time.

She pauses, then lets out a humorless laugh. "That's assuming I still want you, prick."

"Ah. Good to see you're finally admitting you wanted me," I drawl. "And giving me my first pet name all in the same sentence. How did I ever get so lucky?"

Her nails scrape down my skin so roughly I wouldn't be surprised if I was bleeding. "Perhaps asshole is more fitting," she muses. "Maybe cock-blocking, ass-eating, fuckface is—"

"Feel me, Addy," I breathe, cutting off her adorable tirade as I rub my thumb over her hip in soothing strokes. "Don't think. Don't question this. Just fucking *feel me*. For once in your goddamned life—turn off that beautiful brain of yours and just exist with me.

In response to my words, her entire body shudders. It takes her a moment to give in and even longer to fully sink into me, but when she does, I feel as though I've just won the lottery. At 6'0, I'm a moderately tall guy, but with Addy wearing sky-scrapper heels, she's nearly evenly matched with me. So, when her head tips back, she's at the perfect height to rest it on my shoulder, granting me full access to her long, swan-line neck. Access I plan to take full advantage of.

The crowd parts as some people drift away from the glory hole scene in favor of the St. Andrews Cross that, now has a female/female couple taking advantage of the whip and bondage selection. I hedge Addy forward a few steps, never releasing her, so we can get a better view of the thrupple in front of us.

The red-heeled woman's been flipped onto her back at some point, and the two men playing with her have strapped her ankles to leather shackles suspended from the ceiling, spreading her wide open. Despite the voyeuristic situation, it's clear to see the care the two men have, not only for each other but for the woman they're pleasuring. They may all be buck ass naked in front of a crowd of strangers, but they aren't putting on a show for us. They're enjoying the fuck out of themselves and getting what I'd suspect is a healthy dose of adrenaline by being here.

"Were they hired for the party?" Addy whispers, her eyes locked on where the taller man is bent over the woman's body as much as possible, gripping her hips through the tiny box and pounding into her wet cunt ruthlessly. The second man, a shorter, stockier guy, is taking full advantage of his partner's bent-over position as he preps his ass with a thin glass dildo covered in shiny lube.

My lips trail up Addison's neck. She smells sweet, like sugar and vanilla, with a hint of musk. It's intoxicating, and I can't help but roll my tongue across her skin, getting a taste of her sweetness. "No," I murmur, my lips tickling her sensitive flesh, causing her to shiver. "They're just like us, baby. Here for the party."

"Don't call me that," she mumbles, her hand flexing on my arm. I chuckle. "What do you mean?" she asks, returning to my previous statement. "We're all just free to touch and fuck whoever we want?"

Acid pools in my stomach at the idea of her *touching* and *fucking* anyone but me, but I won't lie to her. I may have gotten the inside scoop about the party and what the event planners' ideas for this evening were well before they were made public, thanks to my inside source. He hacked the system easily enough, finding the guest list, itinerary, and information in less than an hour, giving me all the ammo I'd need to make tonight work in my favor. A fact I refuse to be ashamed of.

"Yes," I exhale before licking the shell of her ear. "It's a free for all tonight. Anything you want. Anything your heart," I pause, trailing my hand up her too-thin waist and placing my palm right over her heart. It thumps erratically beneath my skin as I bring my lips to her ear, letting her feel my warm breath. "*Desires is yours,*" I whisper.

She shudders but doesn't speak or move away from my touch, so I continue. I drift down her body, stopping only briefly to graze her soft breasts in a teasing touch. I trail down, down, *down* before boldly cupping her cunt through her dress. She sucks in a sharp breath and shifts backward, grinding her sweet ass into my already throbbing cock. "Anything this pretty pussy desires is yours." Unable to help myself, I grind my palm against her clit softly, not giving her the friction she needs but letting her see my intent.

Addison Hughes may not know it yet, but she's mine. Body, mind, heart, and fucking soul, and I'll prove it to her, one mind-blowing orgasm at a time.

Even if she fights me every step of the way.

Chapter Five

Addison

Sex is an interesting thing for me. I've always been a sexual person. At first, I'd used it as an escape method in my late teens and early twenties while in college. It was the first time I'd been *allowed* away from home for any extended period of time, and suffice it to say, I'd gone wild. Absolutely, recklessly wild.

What can you expect? Being the daughter of one of the wealthiest families in Colorado...well...not quite. Though my parents, primarily my father, are incredibly rich, their wealth is nothing next to the billionaire Nicolai Saint who only recently got rid of his toy store empire. Even with the ownership transfer, he's still sickeningly rich. Unlike my family, I hear Nicolai is actually a good man, but I digress. Point is: my father, Howard Hughes, is a self-made millionaire, and therefore, my mother is by proxy, who, after living a life of hardship in a trailer park, took to money like a fish to water. She soaked up the lifestyle like a sponge and forced it down my throat every chance she got.

So—when I rebelled, I rebelled *good*.

I learned very quickly in my sexual exploration that there wasn't much I wouldn't try at least once. I also discovered that through sex, particularly times when I would be in charge, or topping, I was able to become the most comfortable, confident, and *brave* version of myself. I clung to that knowledge, researched, tested the theory, and ran with it. Ten years later, I'm a 34-year-old Domme who comes alive in the bedroom and confidently dominates it the way I do the courtroom.

How-the-fuck-ever…one minute in Jackson Lowell's arms, and I'm ready to drop to my knees, grip his thighs and beg him to fuck my throat while crying, *"Yes, Daddy. I'd like some more, Daddy."* It's jarring and terrifying. That's why I ran all those months ago. I saw him and his potential to ruin me, and I got scared. He gave me an inch, and I, quite literally, took a mile. Many, many miles. A decision that I regretted immediately. But I stand by it. I have to. Otherwise…well, otherwise, he might really see me. And if he does, he'll leave like everyone else. He'll judge me like everyone else.

He'll hurt me like everyone else.

I swallow thickly, the thought bringing me back to the present. His lips are trailing down my neck and shoulder at a torturously slow pace as he grinds his palm into my clit with more pressure than before. I gasp, my hips shooting forward as pleasure races through my body, clouding my mind. I couldn't deny the chemistry between Jack and me even if I wanted to. It's obvious. I'm drawn to him in a way I've never been drawn to anyone before. I want him with every cell in my body and fiber of my being. Maybe that's why...just this once, just this moment, I let go and sink into him.

My head drops back onto his shoulder as I roll my hips in a slow, sensual rhythm. With every sway, I grind my throbbing clit against his big hand, and with every ebb, my ass bounces off his even bigger cock. He chuckles, the sound muffled in the crook of my neck, but I can hear the hint of pain and arousal in his thick, deep voice. I smile proudly, enjoying the fact that I can torture him the same way he's torturing me. My tiny lacy thong is soaked, and he's barely just begun. It's only right to make him walk around with a massive hard-on. Except, the thought causes the little green monster inside of me to rear its ugly head.

That can't be right. I don't care who looks at Jack's dick or touches him. Hell, he can fuck who—*nope*. Absolutely not going down that road.

Desperate to shake the angry, jealous thoughts away, I tilt my head to the side, seeking his mouth, knowing it'll send me over the edge. Catching him off guard, the pressure against my clit disappears, and his head rears back. I growl, my brows furrowed. Jack's lip tips up mockingly as he cocks his head to the side. His beautiful green eyes twinkle in the low lighting, holding me captive as he slowly slips his hand up my sensitive inner thigh, dipping below my short dress. His dark blonde brow arches with a challenge.

I tuck my lips between my teeth, taking his challenge on and upping the ante. Just as the pads of his fingers reach my soaked panties and graze over my swollen lips, I reach back and grip his hard cock. His hips buck, and he sucks in a breath. I smirk, arching my own brows. Jack growls, and before I realize what's happening, he's shoved my panties aside and, with more accuracy than I'd think possible, shoves two thick fingers into my aching pussy. I barely stifle a scream. My hand flexes without thought, gripping his large erection through his slacks.

"What are you going to do now, Jackson?" I breathe. My mouth is dry as a dessert causing me to lick my lips. His eyes follow the movement and flare with something dark and possessive. My pussy clenches around his unmoving fingers. My hips are demanding that I ride his hand, but I stay still, refusing to be the first to move. We stand there in the middle of a crowd, surrounded by muffled moans, loud grunts, and even louder screams of pleasure. Sex and debauchery are happening all around us, mingling with fancy appetizers and well-dressed strangers, yet the only thing I can see is *him*. The only thing I can feel is *him*.

Jackson Fucking Lowell.

Chapter Six

Addison

WE STARE AT ONE another, waiting to see who'll break first. I'm slightly preoccupied fighting with the internal need to check him out, like always. A cursory glance shows me he's dressed more casually than most of the men here, yet he stands out as though he's a goddamned GQ model.

In form-fitting black slacks that cover his long, muscular legs like a second skin, I've no doubt his ass looks delectable in. The black button-down he's wearing is just as tight, showing off his strong chest and broad shoulders. Jack isn't a huge guy. I've always imagined that he has more of a swimmer's body than anything. He's taller than I am, at around 6'0. He works out daily. I know because I used to accidentally see him return to work and head to his in-office shower after lunch in his soiled gym clothes, looking like a fucking snack.

Okay. It wasn't an accident. I perved and stalked him. Even went as far as waiting at the reception desk casually at 1:04 pm for the sweaty show. Every day. Can you blame me?

God, I miss sharing an office with him.

My mouth waters, and I force my gaze back to his face. His eyes are bright green with gold flecks. His hair is dark blonde and slicked back loosely in a haphazard style that screams *I spent eight hours making it look this messy.* My mind filters through images of ways I can truly mess it up. His skin is light, like mine, but there's a dusting of reddish freckles across his nose that I find utterly adorable. His jaw and cheekbones are chiseled and bare. I don't think I've ever seen Jack with facial hair. In fact, besides the afternoons after the gym, I don't think I've ever seen the man even slightly undone.

He's polite, put-together, and clean-cut. It's easy to see, with just a quick glance, that he comes from a background of privilege like myself. Yet, he's so damn kind; he lacks the inherent uppity behavior you'd expect from someone raised with immense wealth.

Jack smirks at me, tilting his pretty face to the side and bringing me back to the present. "Checking me out, Addy?" he murmurs heatedly.

Holy shit—have I just been standing here gaping at the man with my hand wrapped around his junk? Fuck.

Growling, I squeeze his dick again, not giving in to the need to yank his slacks down and let him fuck my fist and face. All of his previous cocky swagger disappears in an instant at the unspoken threat. Jackson leans forward, bringing his mouth less than an inch from mine. My heart rate spikes and my eyes drop down to his lips as the importance of this moment spears through me.

It dawns on me then... we've flirted. We've talked a big game. Our hands are currently touching our most intimate body parts yet—we've never even kissed. And God, how badly I want to kiss him.

This is it. This is it. This is it—my brain chants causing my heart to beat inexplicably faster and my pussy to throb around his fingers. Jack swallows thickly and closes the distance between us. *3, 2—*

"Watch the fucking show like the obedient little slut I know you can be, and I'll reward you." His lips ghost over mine with every word, distracting me. That's the only excuse I have for the momentary delay in my reaction.

Then, his words finally trickle in and hit me. My eyes slam open. *When had they closed?* Anger and frustration skyrockets inside of me, replacing some of the giddy feelings I'd stupidly let fill me just seconds ago. My hand squeezes his dick so hard I'm surprised I don't yank it off. He grunts and winces, trying to pull away from me. I yank again and release him, jerking away. His fingers slip from my pussy as I take a step away, putting some much-needed distance between us. I'm surprised when I realize that despite my mental and emotional reaction to his words, my body is still dripping with excitement and arousal...*for him.*

"What the fuck, Addy?" he barks, palming his dick.

I adjust my dress as everything around us slowly begins to trickle in. Some people closest to us smile, completely unrepentant of the fact that they'd been watching our battle of wills. I shake my head and roll my shoulders back, turning to meet his eyes. His jaw ticks, and he takes a step toward me. I shake my head. My emotions are all over the place in a direct, painful contradiction to my body.

I straighten my spine.

Jack pales.

"*Don't do this, Addison.*"

It's the plea in his voice that has me freezing in confusion. He wastes no time stepping into my space again. His hand is around my throat in the next second, shocking me even more. His forehead hits mine. "Don't," he repeats, sounding pissed off and, even more surprisingly, *hurt*.

"Don't what?" I whisper though I think I already know. And if I'm right, it's even more of a reason to run right now.

"Don't pull away from me. Don't go back behind that fucking fortress. Let me in, goddammit. Please*." He sees me*. It's my biggest fear and my deepest wish. It's too much. I open my mouth, but he shakes his head once. "No. Just listen to me. I know you, Addison Hughes. I've known you for years. I know you more than you know yourself and more than you'd ever willingly let someone."

My eyes squeeze shut as fear and embarrassment wash over me, mixing with an unhealthy dose of denial.

He can't.

"I *know* you, and I'm still here. I want you. I want you so fucking bad that I'm dying without you. Do you understand that? I see you, and I want you even more because of it. *Stop running.*" His breathing is labored. There's a slight tremble to his usually calm body. It's overwhelming. Intoxicating. Everything.

I swallow thickly. My fingers find his button-down shirt and tangle in the fabric, twisting it roughly. I'm not sure if I'm trying to pull him into me or push him away. "I can't," I murmur. This time, I'm the one to shush him when he tries to interrupt. My heart is thudding at an erratic staccato, and my hands are trembling as badly as his body. My stomach is twisting so harshly that I'm afraid I might puke all over his shiny shoes, which is saying something, considering I haven't eaten today. I was too nervous. *Good thing, too.* "I'm damaged, Jackson. I'm broken inside. I have," I swallow again, nearly choking on the bile in my throat. "*Monsters,*" I practically spit the word.

"So do I," he cuts in before I can stop him.

I lean back, finally meeting his beautiful eyes. His hand flexes around my throat, and the other wraps around my cheek softly. It's like he's warring with his two sides of himself. Sides I'm not sure many others see. But not many others pay as close attention to Jack as I do. They see his humor. His professionalism. His kindness. His background. They know who his family is. They have expectations and assumptions. I have the real him. I see the lighthearted man that everyone else sees, but I also see his darkness. His anger and frustration. The depravity. The possessiveness. A part of me wonders if I only see it because it's there for me.

I quickly dismiss the thought.

Stupid dreams.

Jack palms my cheek roughly, dragging my face where he wants me. He presses his lips to my forehead in a move that has my heart clenching painfully. His lips ghost across my skin as he murmurs, "I have monsters too, Addison. I'll dance with yours if you dance with mine."

I shake my head with a scoff. "I'm so confused right now. This is so much. It's out of nowhere," I choke out, trying to pull away. The hand around my throat tightens, and I gasp for breath.

"That's bullshit," he growls, his eyes burning in a glower. "This isn't out of nowhere, and we both know it. *Just fucking give in.* Let yourself feel this. Us. Just for one night, and if you still don't think there's anything between us tomorrow, I'll walk away." He swallows, squeezing his eyes shut like the thought is painful. My own heart squeezes like the very fist wrapped around my throat is around the stupid organ in my chest as well.

Could I do that? Give into him. Just once. One night and then we walk away. We give into the lust and chemistry between us. Then, he'll see I'm nothing more than a pretty body and walk away like everyone else.

No, he won't, my brain whispers. I shut the needy bitch up and smirk up at him, faking it the way I do everything else in my life. "Fine," I agree, knowing damn well he'll walk away tomorrow, and I'll be left nursing my wounded ego and a broken heart. His eyes gape in shock.

"But you'll have to work for it." His hand slips away, an adorable, confused look replacing his shock. I bring my colorful arm up, waving it in front of his face. "I still have other options, don't I?" I chuckle, taking a step back with a shrug, shoving away all the deep emotions I can't deal with and embracing my alter-ego like a second skin. "If you're the last man standing, I'm all yours."

It takes him a few seconds to catch up, but when he does, he grins back at me wickedly. The look is so devilish on his handsome, chiseled face that I actually shiver. Locking eyes with me, Jack brings his fingers up to his mouth and slowly, *so fucking slowly*, sucks them between his thick lips. I choke when I realize he's sucking on the fingers that he'd had inside me. Even worse, he's *moaning* with his eyes closed like I'm the best thing he's ever tasted.

His fingers slip from his mouth in a sensual move before he murmurs, *"Fucking delicious, Princess."* This time, I do choke. Jack smirks. "Game fucking on."

A waiter passes at that exact moment with a tray of shots. I pick up the clear double shooter and toss it back. Tequila. Shrugging confidently as though I'm not burning from the inside out, I turn on my heel and head toward the next display, calling over my shoulder, "For one night only."

Famous last words.

Chapter Seven

jackson

THIS LITTLE FUCKING BRAT.

I know exactly what she's doing. No one speaks Addison Hughes better than I do. I probably speak her language better than she does, which is the exact reason we're in this situation. She's scared. I get it. I am too. But I meant what I said. I'm not the choir boy people think I am. I may go to church, but it's got a hell of a lot less to do with religion than it does with me, hoping the ugly demons inside of me will be exorcized just by proximity to the cross than anything else.

My cock is throbbing, my chest feels like I got rammed by a bull, and the lusty fog surrounding me refuses to clear as I watch her cute little ass sway away from me. Her head cocks to the side, and she slows to a stop at the display next to the female glory hole. I chuckle when I realize what has her so interested.

A quick scan around the vast space shows me that some people have left since we were caught in our own little world. Likely upstairs to the suites. From what I know, all the rooms are stocked with the same items and equipped for a night of your wildest fantasies. If they're missing something you want, within reason, it's likely in the store off the back side of the party room we're in. Couples or partners can call down and have it brought up by staff. Talk about room service. They also supply food, drinks, condoms, liquor, lube, etc. It's an incredible idea, in my opinion. Talk about a money-maker. Nothing sells like sex. Literally.

I grin to myself as I trail slowly behind Addy. The fewer people that are still standing, the less likely she is to talk to or choose any of her other matches. An idea forms in my mind. All I need to do is keep her distracted until everyone else has paired off. *You're really losing it, Jack.* A loud male laugh draws my attention from my perfect view of my girl, and I find a big, bulky, attractive dude a few feet away, laughing with a woman. My eyes find both of their wrists, and unsurprisingly, they have matching yellow bracelets. The woman only has one other, a bright blue. The man, however, has five total. My gaze snags on a dark green one with yellow stripes.

One that identically matches one of Addison's.

Irritation has me growling out a feral as fuck sound. The poor woman directly to my left jumps and spills her champagne down her dress before shooting me a terrified look. *Fucking hell.* "Shit, sorry," I murmur, palming the back of my neck uncomfortably.

Before I can do anything, like stupidly cleaning up the spill like a creep, a man with a bold, fluorescent orange bracelet waves me away with a harsh glare and turns to the woman, hearts in his eyes. She glances from his bracelet to hers, finding them matching, and blushes wildly. *Jesus fucking Christ.* It's like mating season around here. Everyone's khuis are resonating left and right. I shake my head with a smile. I should never have joined that damn book club with Rayvn and her friend Shiloh. Biting my lip, I step up behind Addy. That Ice Planet Barbarian was a damn good book, though. Wish I had a nub of my own for double penetration. Would make things a lot easier.

Addy gasps, pulling my attention from my wayward, chaotic thoughts. Various scenes break up the room. The first, when you enter, was the female glory hole, meant for a woman to be partially hidden while participants play with her how they choose. The second is the opposite. A fact that's made clear when the small hole in the wall is suddenly filled with a long, stiff cock. It looks so crass and yet beautiful next to the elegant wallpaper. There's a gold, filigree-designed metal contraption around the hole, making it stand out and soften the edges. There are small tables on either side of the hole, with various toys and instruments to make playing more interesting. There are even cushions on the floor just beneath the hole.

Curious, I scan the wall, looking for some sort of doorway where partygoers can enter to get into position for the holes. Sure enough, between the two displays is a thick door with a sign that says, *Enter Gloryhole Here.* When we filled out our applications, we all agreed that if we chose to participate in a public scene, we were consenting to a free for all. It's hard to monitor everyone's dos and don'ts in such a public setting, but safewords are used for every situation. On top of that, protection and STD tests were gone over thoroughly before entry was granted.

Turning back to Addy, my cock throbs in time with my heart and the low bass of the sexy, smooth music playing in the background. It's easy to lose yourself in a place like this. But right now, every part of me is homed in on the beautiful blonde in front of me as she searches the room, her lip tucked between her teeth. I stand silently, a few feet behind her. Her eyes widen when she spots me. I see her throat bob with a swallow. Then, the little brat smirks and steps forward, effectively entering the scene space.

Oh, fuck.

Chapter Eight

jackson

I TRY, I REALLY try, to keep my panic under wraps. She said I needed to earn her. Said I needed to be the last man standing. She's testing me. Wanting to see how far I'll go for her. Silly, pretty thing is deluded if she hasn't realized it yet. I'd go to the ends of the earth for my girl and then throw myself over the edge if she demanded it. So, it's no surprise that I follow when she drops to her knees in front of the lonely, hard cock poking through the glory hole without a word. She primly settles herself on the floor cushions as though it's a throne instead of a pillow in front of a stranger's dick.

Shaking myself from my stupor, I close the few feet between us, stepping up to her side. Addy looks up at me, and all the blood in my body rushes straight to my already hard cock at the sight of her on her knees. She may be inches from someone else's cock, but it's me she's looking at.

My mouth salivates at the vision. Perfect, elegant, beautiful Addison. Knees spread slightly, pale cheeks flush, blue eyes glazed and bright as she stares up at me with a doe-eyed yet sultry look. She naturally has the expression every pornstar hopes to perfect, and every man dreams about. It's effortless on her, and my own knees grow weak at the sight.

"*Fuck me*," I breathe, my voice raspy and pained.

Her eyes widen a fraction. She exhales in a rush before smirking, and I already know I'll both love and hate the next words out of her mouth. "No thanks," she murmurs, licking her thick, pouty lips. "I think I'll fuck him instead."

And then, her pink mouth wraps around the stranger's cock with zero hesitation. My eyes gape, and this time, my knees do waver. Quickly, I catch myself on the table next to me before I fall to the ground. Toys clatter in the *clean* and *soiled* bins just as I hear a distinctly masculine shout through the wall that surprisingly has me chuckling. But then, my girl's eyes drift closed in ecstasy, and everything shifts.

No. Hell no.

My hand darts out and wraps around her long ponytail. I fist it, yanking her head back as I bend down to meet her wide, shocked eyes. She whimpers, and I click my tongue in disapproval. "If you wanna play, Princess, we'll play. I'll let you suck that cock like the cum thirsty whore you are, but you keep those big, beautiful blue eyes on me. Do you understand?"

Her lips are still wrapped around the man's dick, and despite the wall between them, he's trying to thrust the long, pretty appendage down my girl's throat. It takes Addy a second to recover, but when she does, she leans back and pops off his cock with an audible slurp that has precum leaking from my tip. I groan as my eyes flutter.

"*Let me?*" she hisses, anger and venom spilling from her mouth like fire. I blink at her. She laughs sarcastically. "Let's get one thing straight, Jackson," she growls, trying to bat my hand away from the grip on her hair. I double down, wrapping it around my fist in a relentless hold. "If anyone is in charge here, it's me. If I want to suck his cock, I will, and I'll do it however I damn well, please. You're the one who started this game. I'm the one winning it."

My brows lift so high they're practically in my slicked-back blonde hair. Oh, she wants to play like that, does she? A deep, rumbling laugh erupts from my throat. Using the tight grip on her hair, I lead her forward until her lips are touching his tip, that's now red and throbbing with need. Bending further, I find her ear.

"Suck it and suck it good. Put on a show for everyone. Make them so mad with lust, they have no choice but to stick their hands in their pants and fuck themselves to the sight of you." She hesitates at my harsh growl, but I'm done fucking around. She wants to fight me. She wants to scare me away. I'll show her that I can take her monsters, dominate them—wring orgasm after orgasm from them until they're begging for more. And then, I'll do it all over again, making sure she's so damn satisfied she can't remember a time when she questioned me.

"*Now, Addison.*" I shove her roughly until she's forced to open her mouth. She does it begrudgingly, all the while glaring at me like she wishes I'd wither up and die on the spot.

I chuckle darkly. "Let's be real, Princess," I coo, using a nickname that rolls off my tongue as though it was always meant to belong to her. "If you didn't want to suck his dick…If you didn't want to let me force you, I'd be on my ass. You crave this. You need it. You may act like a hardass bitch to everyone you know, but *I see you.*" I hiss the last words, emphasizing them as I control her bobbing motions up and down this stranger's cock.

Her hips shift, and her thighs rub together as she searches for friction. I chuckle again, palming her heavy tit in a way that's likely degrading, but I know turns her on. I read her profile up and fucking down. I have that shit memorized. I know what she wants, what she likes. I also know what she only admitted on a blank, private form, thinking no one else would see it. My head runs through her profile for the hundredth time.

Female Dominant seeking:
Submissive, Switch, Male Dominant
Activities of Interest:
Anal/Giving/Receiving, Blindfold/Gagging, Biting, Bondage-Light, Choking, Collars/Wearing, Collaring Submissive, Cuckholding/Sharing, Degradation with praise, Double Penetration, Face Slapping, Forced Orgasms, Hair Pulling, HandCuffs, Head/Giving/Receiving, Humiliation in Public/Private-Light, Impact Play/Hands only, Rigging/Rope Play, Sex in Scene/Public

Sex, Spanking, Spit Play, Strap-on's/Pegging, Voyeurism/Exhibitionism

I also have her limits and medical form memorized. I should feel guilty, but seeing her come to life right now, wrapped around some stranger's cock while I control her—it's beautiful. And so damn worth it.

Addy likes to call herself a Domme, and don't get me wrong—I know she is. I know she's good at it, and I have every fucking intention of letting her top me. But I also know what she craves deep down. What she's too scared to ask for. Too terrified of what it'll mean. She wants to be vulnerable. She wants to give up that cool, calm, controlled façade she works so damn hard to keep up all day, every day. And to do that, she needs to trust someone else to take care of her. To keep her safe. She needs to let go and give in.

She needs a *home*. I'll be that for her and so much more if she'll let me. I'll give her every single thing she wants and protect her like the precious gift she is.

"Look at you," I breathe, running my thumb across her pink cheek. "You're fucking starving for it. If I dipped my hand between your pretty little thighs, you'd be soaked, wouldn't you? You'd be a sloppy, wet mess."

Tears coat her cheeks from my rough control, especially when I shove her down deep on the cock she's eagerly slurping. Her hands stay primly rested on her thighs. She doesn't try to brace herself or stop me. She's not new to this world. She knows all she'd have to do is tap my leg or hand, and this would be over. But she doesn't.

Fuck. That simple act of submission makes me so proud of my girl.

I smile, loosening my hold. I stroke her wet cheek with my other hand soothingly, wiping away her messy tears and smearing her mascara. "That's it," I praise. She's so damn beautiful. So perfect. "Choke on it like my good girl. You can do it, Princess."

I loosen my hand even further, giving her free reign. Testing her. She swallows around his dick, and another muffled shout comes from the other side of the wall. Addy locks eyes with me, reaches up, and tightens my hold on her hair before leaning in and deepthroating his cock to the point that she does, indeed, choke and sputter.

There.

There it is.

Agreement. Permission. Acceptance.

Holy Shit.

Chapter Nine

E VERYTHING. THIS IS EVERYTHING.

I press my lips to the top of her head. My eyes close against my will as relief rushes through me. I breathe her addicting scent in and kiss her sweetly. It's only a second. One moment of contentment. Of gratitude and praise. Then, I fist her hair and rip her off his dick, pushing her back gently to make space. She coughs and gags, wiping at her face frantically. Suddenly, the lust has disappeared from her blissed-out face. Her eyes are huge, and anger radiates off her palpably.

"What the fuck, Jackson," she growls in a broken, rough voice.

Okay. Well—that was short-lived.

Sighing, I resist the urge to rub my forehead. The man on the other side of the wall cries out in frustration, and I'm pretty sure he punches the wall. I bark a laugh at the pair of them whining and upset. Smirking, I drop to my knees next to Addy, lock eyes with her, and lick a slow, torturous path up the dripping, long cock as though it's my own personal lollypop. He bucks again, groaning. As if to chastise him, I flick his throbbing tip, and he jerks. Addy gasps as I wrap my lips around the red and angry mushroom head, unable to hold back the moan at their combined flavor.

My lips slide down his cock, and my hands ache with the need to grip his thighs and roll his heavy sac in my palm. Instead, my gaze finds Addison's, and surprisingly, not only are her blue eyes locked on my mouth, but her hand is working a quick path down her body, between her thighs. I growl in irritation and pop off the poor guy's dick once more. He slams the wall and starts to withdraw his cock. My hand snaps out, gripping it harshly.

"Relax," I bark, loud enough that he should be able to hear me. He freezes. "Thank you," I praise, my eyes still locked on Addy as I speak to him. "You'll get to cum soon. I promise. Reach down and fist your balls for me. Hold off as long as you can. We're almost there." I see a shadow move from the small space surrounding his cock, letting me see the guy's hand move down his body and cup his balls. I lick his tip, sucking hard, before popping off again. "Such a good fucking boy for me."

He groans. I smirk and shift, turning to face the assortment of fresh toys. I pluck one that I'd spotted earlier from the bin and toss it to Addy. "What's this?" she asks, even though we both know she's perfectly aware she's holding a clit sucking vibrator.

I grin at her in a way that's more evil than sweet. "Legs spread. Panties to the side. Show me how wet that pretty little pussy is for me, Princess." She hesitates, her brows dipping. Observing her, I watch with rapt attention as she tugs her lip between her teeth and looks away awkwardly.

Ducking around the protruding wall-cock, I find her face and drag it back to me. I palm her jaw and shove my thumb between her lips. "Do what I fucking said, Addison or I swear to God, I will keep you on edge for so fucking long, you'll be begging me to walk away, just so you can have some relief." She bites down on my thumb and stares at me. I nod approvingly. "There she is. There's my feisty little bitch. Now do it."

I slip my thumb from her mouth, shivering when she refuses to release me and ends up scraping her teeth down my flesh, deep enough to draw blood. Good. That's what I want. The harder she fights, the better her ultimate submission will be.

I wait her out, mentally counting down the seconds it takes her to listen. Less than thirty. That's how long it takes her to spread her bent thighs wide, ruck up her tiny dress, yank her barely there black thong to the side, and grant me my first sight of her dripping, pink cunt. My mouth waters immediately, and I groan loudly. I want to devour her. Feast on her right here and now in front of God and all his witnesses, but I can't. Once I start, I won't stop, and while I'm down with exhibitionism, I will not allow our first time to be in front of all these people. Because when I finally get inside Addison Hughes, it'll be more than a quick fuck. It'll be the start of forever.

"So pretty," I purr. "So perfect for me." She swallows roughly. "Vibrator on your clit. You don't cum until I tell you to. You don't look away. Eyes on me. Understood?" She gives me a jerky nod. I cock a brow. "I think I'd like to hear you say it, Princess."

She rolls her eyes, and I barely stifle a bark of laughter. I'm not huge into physical punishments, but something tells me Addy will change that. "Yes, Sir," she mutters angrily, and my balls draw up as precum shoots from my tip.

Fuck.

I try to hide my shock but must not catch it fast enough. She smirks proudly and blinks rapidly, feigning innocence. My dick throbs and my heart squeezes at the mixture of slutty and adorable she's displaying. Jesus. She's perfect. The vibrator clicks on, and her middle bows, but she doesn't look away. Confident that she'll do her job, I go back to mine.

My lips wrap around the cock that's sadly but understandably wilted slightly. Doesn't matter. I'll reward him. He earned it. My hand wraps around the base of his length, drawing his flesh forward as my mouth slides down, making sure to keep every inch of him covered with my warmth. I cradle the underside of his shaft with my tongue, paying attention to the sensitive vein I'm tracing. He shudders. Addison moans loudly, and he jerks in my hand.

I should be mad that he's getting off to the sound of my girl's pleasure, but the realization that she and I are doing this to him together, bringing him ecstasy as a team, hits hard. At this moment, with her eyes locked on mine, I own her. She's mine. Every other man and woman in this room could be watching, stroking themselves, fucking to the sight of us—but she's still *mine*. That thought has me doubling down in my efforts.

My balls are aching painfully. My cock has never been harder, and if I didn't know any better, I'd say I'm just as close to cumming as the pair of them. Addy is shaking. Her cheeks are pink. Her eyes are clouded with lust. The vibrator is trembling in her hand, and her hips are rocking at a quick pace. I jerk the man faster, sucking his tip with vigor. My teeth scrape across his already taut skin, and I know he's close. I time his orgasm with Addison's. When I see her unable to hold herself back any longer, I give her a tiny nod. Her scream penetrates the air and sets him off. Hot, salty cum coats my tongue, filling my mouth jet after jet. I take it all, never losing sight of Addy as she rides the aftershocks of her orgasm. Her entire body is flush and twitching.

She's stunning. Fucking incredible.

When his cock finally relents in my mouth, I slip off. He immediately drops back, leaving us, and I crawl across the concrete floor to Addy. I reach her just as she tosses the vibrator aside, still shaking. Her eyes are dazed and happy as she looks up at me.

Beautiful.

Mine.

Knee to knee, I arch over her, gripping her throat with one hand making her eyes widen. I squeeze and then slide up, palming her face. Applying pressure to her cheeks, I force her mouth open. She sucks in a breath, and I waste no time spitting the stranger's load onto her tongue. I can tell she's shocked and angry. But I can also hear the heady whimper she tries to hide. I watch, entranced, as her mouth fills with foamy, white liquid.

Me. Him. Her.

"Swallow," I rasp, releasing her. Glaring, she does as I've commanded. "My perfect girl," I murmur, undeniably obsessed with Addison Hughes. *Lowell has a nice ring to it.*

Her face pinches as she slides her legs closed and fixes her dress. "I'm not your anything." My jaw flexes, and I get ready to call her out, but she shakes her head, climbs to her feet, and steps away. "Unless you have short-term memory loss, you can't possibly have forgotten the terms of our deal." She shows me her bracelets with a shaky arm. "I still have men to meet." Her eyes flick to my single bracelet, and she chuckles. "Shouldn't have been so cocky."

"Lose them, Addison," I snap, jumping up. "Take them off. You already know who you belong to."

She wavers but shakes it off. "I belong to no one, Jackson. Especially not you." And with that, she turns away, immediately seeking out one of her other matches.

Another man.

Another opportunity with someone who isn't me.

Shit.

Chapter Ten

Addison

WHAT IS THIS VOODOO magic? *Holy shit.* I feel like I'm only seconds from passing out due to blood loss. Blood loss because it's all currently residing in my clit like it's trying to make a tiny little boner for everyone to see.

I exhale a shaky breath, trying desperately to shake myself from whatever the hell *that* was. My eyes scan the party, finding nearly half of the original attendees missing. I check the tiny gold watch on my wrist and almost choke when I realize I've already been here for an hour and a half. My gaze catches the bracelets stacked up around my watch, and a pang hits me right in the gut at the sight of them. Every part of me wants to look over my shoulder and seek out Jackson. My mouth still tastes like cum mixed with a flavor that I'm assuming is all Jack. Assuming because despite what we just did, the man still hasn't kissed me.

I scoff, crossing my arms over my chest as I head deeper into the room. Like I'd even want him to kiss me. *You big fucking liar.* I bite my lip, knowing that, for once, the self-deprecating, ugly voice in my head is completely right.

A sudden realization hits me so hard that I stumble over my heels. From the moment Jack showed up tonight, wrapped around me like he had a right to be there, and everything that transpired after that...my mind has been remarkably empty. I shudder as I replay what just happened with the glory hole, the random dick, Jack...and *me*. Everything he said. Everything he did. His aggressive words and touch. His forcefulness. The degradation. The praise. The exhibitionist act. The way he so easily accepted sharing me.

The kindness. The care.

The way I loved every single second of it.

Fuck. It was incredible. I've done a lot, but that—that was a first for me. My mind was blissfully empty. Like he begged me to do, I let go. Right, wrong or indifferent, I trust Jack implicitly to keep me safe. To know how much I can take. To know what I want. What I *need*.

He really does know me.

My spine pricks and my hands grow clammy as the truth of it barrels into me. Somehow, over the last six years, despite my best effort to keep him and others at a distance, he saw me. Through work functions, late-night meetings, team events, the stress of court, disasters, and casual luncheons…he saw me. He paid attention, and without my permission, he found his way in.

To my world.

My mind.

My stupid, idiotic heart.

Shit.

Desperate to ignore all of that—I force my spine to straighten and enjoy what's left of my night. I've only managed a few steps toward the St. Andrews Cross, where two women are still deep in their erotic, tantalizing scene when someone steps into my path. I blink rapidly at the towering figure who's somehow managed to block out the light surrounding me. My eyes lock on deep brown pits that, for some reason, give me immediate chills. Not the same kind that Jackson gave me, either.

His face is masculine and strong. His skin is tan. His hair black, matching his thick beard. His eyes are brown.

That's it. Those are all the facts I have. All the details I can take in. Everything beyond that escapes me as his hand reaches out and wraps around my thin wrist, dwarfing it. I panic, jerking back as my heart thunders. His eyes widen, and he throws his hands up, taking a step back. "Woah," he rumbles, his voice a deep baritone. "I'm sorry to scare you, beautiful. I just wanted to check."

I swallow rocks, still dazed over everything that happened with Jack, including my recent revelation. "Check?" I mumble. *Fuck, Addy. Get it together. Grow up. You can speak to a man.* He nods, grinning, and points to my arm. I follow his gaze and instantly deflate when I realize what he's referring to. "My bracelets," I state.

"Yep." He pops the *p* with an awkward chuckle. I find his face again, seeing his cheeks pink and a slightly bashful look replacing the previous stony expression. It softens me, and I mentally kick myself for being such a freak. "I see we have a match. I knew white would be my lucky color."

I tilt my head to the side, feeling more myself than just moments ago. "Lucky?" I don't miss the tiny purr in my voice. His body reacts to the sound as though I just moaned loudly. He shifts, tilting in my direction until he's practically leaning over me. Well, that accelerated quickly.

"Yep," he says again, his voice deeper. "Look at you. You're everything this bracelet represents."

I blink rapidly once more, this time in shock and confusion. "What does that mean?" My purr has now been replaced with a hiss. Apparently, I'm a fucking cat. A point that doesn't escape assface if his next sentence is anything to go by.

"Ah, Kitten," he laughs, tutting me. "No need to get all feral on me. I just meant you look so innocent with this long, blonde hair and bright blue eyes." His hand reaches up as if to touch my hair, but I jerk away, utterly uncomfortable. Unrepentant, his eyes rake down my body. "A face made by God with a body made by the Devil." He cocks his head to the side, finally returning to my face. "I approve."

Just like that. One look. One declaration, and he thinks I'm his. It's baffling in a way that rocks me to my core. His finger trails a slow path down my forearm, ghosting over the bracelets there, and I shiver, my brain still struggling to keep up. He mistakes the reaction for one of pleasure. Releasing a smug snicker, he grips my wrist again and tugs me forward, using my shock to his advantage. I stumble, catching myself on his chest. His other hand finds my hip, and his lips descend on my neck. Within seconds, he's gotten my much, much smaller body under his control without my permission.

This submission—this touch—is nothing like what I just experienced with Jack. My body burns everywhere he touches, a feeling that's echoed in my mind when he whispers into my ear. The same ear Jack whispered his beautiful, degrading demands earlier. "Come to my room with me, and I'll corrupt you with my cock, Angel."

Okay, one: Ewww. Who says that?

Two: Hell to the no.

The audacity of this prick. My body wants to run. My mouth wants to scream. But my heart is breaking. *I want Jackson.* As soon as the thought hits me, I rear back and bring my knee into the prick's prick...his very hard...very disgusting prick. He growls, shoving me back forcefully. I stumble again, this time into another partygoer. I suck in a breath, thankful for the woman who catches and rights me with a glare at the asshole who pushed me, clearly having seen everything.

Quickly, she whispers, "It's okay. Security is here." It's then that I realize I'm shaking. I watched dazedly as two hulking security guards escort the limping, growling man away. The woman gives me a soft, sad look, then disappears with the crowd, leaving me utterly alone.

What was that? Why? Why do men think they have a fucking right to touch what isn't theirs? The voice in my head chooses that moment to chime in again. *You didn't care when Jack did it.* Overwhelmed, starving, exhausted, and emotionally drained, I suddenly find myself no longer in the mood to party.

My arm tingles where the angry man had gripped me, and I look down, finding already blooming bruises sprouting up on my porcelain skin. Memories of my past, similar injuries, and power plays come to the forefront of my mind. Panic overwhelms me, and I feel myself spiraling down that familiar road. My breaths come in panting bursts, and my hands shake. I ball them up, hiding them against my chest. I blink rapidly, bringing the room back into focus, only to immediately lock eyes on a sight that has me growing dizzy. Acid churns in my empty stomach, causing it to cramp.

Fuck.

I think I might actually pass out. This...this is why I can't get attached. This is why I don't let myself feel.

This is why I ran.

Jackson Lowell—the man who is relentlessly trying to force his way into my soul, my life—currently has a pretty brunette smiling up at him as she drags him into the voyeur box not even ten feet in front of me. In the middle of the expansive room is a glass box that creates a makeshift bedroom. The lighting all around us is dark and minimal, but the box is lit up bright with red spotlights, drawing everyone's attention to a plush red bed sitting in the center of the box. The walls are lined with toys. Whips. Restraints. Dildos.

It's clearly meant for public sex, where everyone can watch but not interact. In any other situation, *literally anything but this*, I'd probably suggest jumping in there and having a good time with someone. Someone like the man currently heading in there with a woman that isn't me.

As it stands, all I can bring myself to do right now is choke down the vomit in my throat and suppress the sob building in my lungs.

Black spots fill my vision, and without a second thought, I do what I always do and run.

Chapter Eleven

jackson

"I TOLD YOU NO," I growl for the umpteenth time, fighting the need to physically push this woman off me. I won't because I don't get rough with women—well, unless they want me to. But also because it's utterly obvious that this woman is drunk as hell.

She pouts up at me, the same way she did the last time I denied her advances. I sigh and look around me for help. Maybe a manager or someone can get her a room to sleep it off. It's not safe for her to be alone in a room full of horny men.

All thoughts of the drunk woman disappear, as does everything else when I catch sight of an upset Addison frantically rushing for the elevators that lead to the suites upstairs. I have a moment of heart-wrenching pain as I search for whoever she's with. Relief like

I've never felt before wooshes through my body when I realize she's alone, but it's only brief as concern for my girl trickles in.

Without a second thought, I disentangle the prying woman's fingers from my arms and pass her off to a random woman next to me.

"What the f—" Her eyes widen when she takes in the pouty brunette who, objectively, is cute. Nothing like my Addy, but cute all the same. The lady I pass her off to takes one look at the short, curvy octopus and grins, smoothing her hair back. "Aww, aren't you precious, Love." Something in my brain registers her British accent, but nothing else clicks as I throw her a grateful smile and rush off.

On the way to the elevators, I pass by a staff member and toss a loose finger in the direction I just came from. "There's a small brunette woman beside the Voyeur tank that's really fucking drunk." The waitress bats confused eyes at me, but I don't wait around for her to follow through. I bolt through the straggling, horny, and tipsy partygoers, shoving my way through the heavy double doors that lead upstairs.

The long hallway is bright as hell compared to the dark, red-hued room I just spent the last few hours in, and I have to blink rapidly to fight the burning in my eyes. The sound of the elevator arriving to my left snags my attention, causing my head to whip to the side. A high blonde ponytail swishes as she disappears in the lift. I charge forward, opening my mouth to call out to her but think better of it at the last second. I don't want to give her a reason or warning to push me away.

The door slides closed just as I reach it, but I quickly shove my hand out, catching it at the last second. Slowly, so fucking slowly, the doors part, revealing a tear-stained, pink-cheeked Addison, causing my heart to crumble. I don't pause. I don't speak. I just barrel through the doors, catching her up in my arms before she can protest. She sucks in a sharp breath, and the elevator closes once more before the ascent begins.

"Shh," I whisper, pulling her tense body into me. I have no idea what the fuck happened between the time when I'd seen her flirting with that big mother fucker ten minutes ago and now, but clearly, something did. "I've got you, Addy."

Apparently, that was the wrong thing to say. She shoves me away with a beastly grunt. I could refuse to let her go, but even I know when space is needed, as much as I hate it.

"You've got me?" she snaps, batting her tears away angrily. Huffing out a disbelieving breath, she pushes past me to stand before the doors, crossing her thin arms tightly. "You know," she drawls when my confused silence stretches on too long. "You talk a big game for a man who can't even last five minutes." She shoots a disapproving look over her shoulder, scowling at my dick for some unknown reason.

Before I can ask what the hell she's going on about, the door slides open, and Addy gracefully exists, her head held high, her spine rigid. I follow her out without a word, unwilling to let her leave my sight, even for a second. Her head swivels back and forth as she tries to find her room. I take note of the floor, realizing it's the same as mine. Wordlessly, I turn her to the right and herd her toward room 36. The room I made sure to stock with every single thing my girl could want and more. All the desires and kinks on her list can be made possible with the contents in my room. But, more than that, it's also their largest suite and the only one with the features it has.

"Where are we going?" she mutters, slightly less combative than seconds ago, like she's deflated.

I have so many questions. So many things I want to say. Number one being: Why the absolute fuck was she running away and crying, and who hurt her? The second being: I will most definitely last longer than five minutes. In fact, I have every intention of fucking her so long and so hard she's unlikely to remember how to speak, let alone complain.

However–I'm pretty sure saying either of those things right now will result in a swift kick to my aching cock, and that's not something I'm willing to risk right now.

My hand skims down her shoulder, her bicep. I find her skin covered in goosebumps and icy to the touch. "To warm you up," I grumble, unable to hide my irritation at her discomfort. She really needs to take better care of herself.

Without my permission, my eyes trail down her body, burning as I note the obvious weight she's lost in the last four months. Addison didn't have weight to lose as it stands. Now, her collarbone and hips are protruding, something I couldn't make out clearly in the dim ballroom. Don't get me wrong. Addy is stunning in any way, shape, form, or size–but seeing someone you care about, someone you love the way I love her–unhealthy and malnourished makes me want to scream and rage.

I bite my tongue so hard I swear it bleeds. Now isn't the time. It will probably never be the time; I know that. I'll just have to take care of her, so there's no question that she's well and healthy.

Nodding to myself, I softly grip her hip to hold her still when we reach our room for the night. I pull my phone from my pocket and scan the code on my invitation with the black glass scanner next to the heavy chrome door.

Addy blinks up at me, eyes narrowed, and shakes her head. "This isn't my room, Jackson." She looks behind, searching the room numbers. "I'm in 2—" The door clicks open, and I gently shove her through the threshold. "Fuck. Do you ever listen? Jesus Christ, Jack. You're the pushiest, bossiest, most persistent arrogant asshole I've ever met."

She's telling me off. Calling me every name in the book. Hissing and fussing and stomping like a toddler. Yet, she's also moving deeper and deeper into the expansive, luxurious room and stripping herself of her shoes—her jewelry—the blasted bracelets on her arm.

Thank God for that.

Leaning against the door, I cock my foot up and cross my arms, perfectly happy to watch her tirade from here. My lip twitches when she grumbles something about *big dicked, perfectly chiseled Greek god of a man-child.* I nearly puff up my chest at that, firmly ignoring the underlying insult.

Finally, she stops rambling and freezes in her tracks. She sucks in a sharp breath and spins in a circle, taking in the room. When I first arrived, hours before the event, I came in to set everything up and make sure it was stocked properly. It really is beautiful, as far as kink rooms in a luxury sex hotel go.

The walls are matte black with a glossy filagree pattern, similar to the one downstairs. The accents are all chrome and sleek, including the massive chandelier suspended from the center of the main room. The ceilings are high, as are the huge windows, currently hidden by heavy black-out curtains. The bed is off to the left against the center of the wall. It's on a raised platform, making it appear regal. It has a solid, sturdy shiny black frame with a built-in hook system for rigging and bondage.

They offer rooms with attached degradation and sex-slave play cages beneath the beds, but I opted out, knowing we wouldn't need it. Don't get me wrong, if my girl really wants to role-play like that someday, I'm down, but not tonight. Tonight is for us, just as we are. Jack and Addy.

The comforter is plush with grey tufts. In front of the floor-to-ceiling windows on the far wall is a large leather drop bench for different positions. Leather straps line the edges for strapping and restraining. To my direct right, the last wall has an ornate wooden and black leather St. Andrews Cross with archaic-looking chain restraints. Through a door next to the bed is the massive en-suite with a large rainfall shower and soaker tub big enough to fit four large people.

I chose this room not only because it's the largest and grandest with the best views—ones we'll be able to appreciate when the sun rises in the morning, but also because it's the only one with a hidden gem hiding just beyond the bathroom. A space I hope she trusts me enough to use tonight.

A harsh chuckle pulls my attention from the opulent room that, with the low lighting, feels more sex dungeon than anything. My head snaps to the center of the room, finding Addy in front of me, mirroring my position. Her tears are long since dried up. Her usual bitchy, annoyed façade firmly in place.

I almost laugh. I know what she's doing. I see right through her. If I had to guess, my woman is feeling a whole hell of a lot right now, and she's trying to hide it. Trying to push me away and protect herself.

Good luck, Princess.

"So, you just thought you'd drag me to your room, and what? Hoped I'd be your willing submissive for the night?" She cackles like her words are the funniest thing she's ever heard.

Smirking, I shake my head, unfolding my arms from my chest as I push off the door. She glares at me, but I see it in her eyes. The anxiety. The panic. I just don't know what exactly she's afraid of.

Is it because she thinks I'll truly force submission on her unwillingly? Is it because she has feelings for me and is afraid to acknowledge them? Does she think she's setting herself up to get hurt?

Unfortunately, I think it's all of the above.

That's exactly why I do what I do next. Ripping my already untucked shirt over my head, I throw it to the side and kick off my shoes before closing the distance between us. Her breathing is labored as she takes in my chest and body for the first time. I don't give her time to explore. She can have that later.

Leaning in, I press my forehead to hers, devouring the sound of her gasp like it's my last meal. "No, Princess. I'm hoping I can be yours," I whisper.

And then, I drop to my knees, bow my head, and exhale a shuddering breath.

"I'm yours to do with as you wish, Mistress."

Chapter Twelve

Addison

IT TAKES ME A stupid amount of time for his words to sink in. I'm so unbelievably overwhelmed right now. I wouldn't be surprised to learn that I'm having some kind of episode. This doesn't feel real. I'm still trying to catch up and wrap my mind around everything that's happened tonight. How did an easy night of sex with a stranger at a Kink party turn into...*this*?

The man I've loved silently from the shadows for years but haven't seen in months is on his knees, giving me not only his permission to do as I please with him but his submission. A man who, up until now, I've known as a bi-sexual Dom that's quiet, reserved, kind, and brilliant.

"Why would you do this for me?" I breathe, too afraid to say the words any louder. My throat is burning as I try to keep a confused sob at bay. I swear I don't usually cry this much. Tonight has been….a lot. Jack doesn't respond, he barely shifts, and my eyes widen in surprise. He's really doing this. Swallowing, I roll my shoulders back and place my hand gently on the top of his head. "Permission to speak," I murmur.

His head bobs slightly but keeps his head bowed and directed at my bare feet, making me wish I'd kept my heels on. In fact, I'm not even sure when I took them off. "I'd do anything for you, Mistress."

The sound of my preferred honorific on his lips hits me square in the gut. It's one thing to give someone a pet name. It's a whole other to refer to them as an honorific. It means something. It's giving absolute trust and devotion. That alone proves how much he cares for me, but his words—they solidify it.

Can I do this with him? Sink into the role where I truly feel like myself? Give him my everything and hope—*pray*—he doesn't change his mind about me? Jack isn't just anyone. He's Jackson…*my Jackson*.

"One night. One night to convince you that what we feel for each other is more than just attraction and chemistry." He shifts, probably fighting the urge to look up at me as I fight a similar urge to run. "Let me show you what you mean to me. Come on. You owe me this, Addison."

The fingers weaving through his hair absently pause and turn to a deathly grip as I wrench his head back without thought. His eyes are wide as he looks up at me. "Try that again, Pet," I demand, my voice lower than he's likely ever heard it before.

Jackson's beautiful green orbs flare with lust, and his tongue pokes out, wetting his lower lip. The sight of him looking up at me, filled with desire, has my core instantly flooding my already-soaked panties. My pussy pulses, achingly aware of how empty I've been all night. *Okay. Maybe I can do this with him.*

"I'm sorry, Mistress," he says softly. I tug his hair harder, causing his neck to bend backward. "I'll do better, Mistress." This time, his words are a low growl that does nothing other than make me want him even more.

Nodding, I decide to say fuck it. If he walks away tomorrow, hopefully, he'll have railed me so hard it at least takes a few days for the heartache to set in.

I release his head, trailing my fingers down his face until I find his lips. They immediately part for me, and I shove two into his mouth, pressing down on his tongue. "Tell me, Pet," I murmur, stepping into him until my pussy is right before his eyes. "Did you enjoy sucking that big cock tonight? Having it down your throat until he filled you with his cum?" His lids flutter closed but quickly snap back open when I slide into his throat. I cock a brow.

Jackson swallows around my fingers, realizing he needs to speak exactly as he is. "Yes. I loved it." His words are muffled, and drool leaks out and down his lips, making me grin.

I slip from his mouth but pause to drag my fingers through the saliva coating us both, making him a sticky mess. If I have it my way, I'll make him a dirty little mess in no time. "Stay like that," I murmur. He doesn't move an inch, pleasing me immensely. He's very good at this, which reminds me. "Have you ever done this before, Jackson?" I ask softly.

He shakes his head. "No. You'll be my first."

My opposite hand finds his jaw, and I can't help but rub soothing strokes across his smooth skin. "You're already doing such a good job for me, Pet. You're a perfect boy for me, aren't you?"

Jack groans, and my pussy throbs. "Only for you, Mistress." His body releases a large shudder. "I'm trying."

I nod, stepping back and letting my hand fall away. "I know you are."

Glancing around the room, I look for inspiration so I can decide how far I want to take this. This isn't like previous scenes I've done. I may be a stone-hard bitch most of the time, but even I'm not callous enough to deny that this here, between Jackson and I, will be different from anything I've encountered. My heart skips a beat. It'll be different because it will mean something.

Everything, my brain whispers. *It'll mean everything.*

Fuck. It will.

But I can't lose myself in those wishful thoughts. I have to stay in control. The first thing I spot surprises me and catches me off guard. I run my fingers over a complex-looking tech system by the front door, but what really drew me here is the large red button that stounds on in the dark room. "What's all this, Pet?"

"The screen is an ordering system in case the room is lacking anything. It's discrete, like a digital shopping platform." My eyes widen, and I glance back at him in question. Jack grins, jutting his chin out. "Anything the room is missing can likely be found in the sex shop downstairs, but they also have a 24/7 kitchen for room service."

"And this?" I ask, running my fingers over the red button.

Jack pauses long enough to have me joining him in the middle of the room once more. He looks worried. "A panic button." My brows furrow. "They try to do their best to keep this place safe and consensual. They screen applicants within an inch of their life, but you can imagine how hard it is to differentiate between consent and non-consent when CNC and dub-con are some people's kinks." Jack shakes his head in anger. "Some people lie, and then it becomes' an attacker's word against a victims."

"Some people are just pieces of shit," I hiss. He nods in agreement.

Jackson's words sink in like a heavy boulder. I understand what he's saying. For as long as I've known about this community, I've also known about the risks. The true kink community is a beautiful place with wonderful, open-minded people. But there are also a ton of disgusting creeps who either don't understand kink properly or who take advantage of situations—something my friend Rayvn knows all too well.

Without thought, my head drops, and my eyes skim the bruise on my wrist. I bet that guy was one of the many people who slip past tests and background checks only to prey on unsuspecting women. I bet he'd even swear up and down that his harsh behavior is consensual. It makes me sick.

"What the fuck is that?" Jack barks, making me jump. My head snaps in his direction, finding him glaring daggers at my injured wrist. It doesn't hurt badly. I just bruise easily, but the sight of him so angry, so worried, on my behalf, does something to me. When I don't respond, he wraps his arm around my hips and drags me into his kneeling body. "Answer me, Addison."

I swallow, petting his head in what I hope is a soothing motion. "I'm fine, Jack."

He growls. Legit growls, and the sound goes straight to my clit. "That's not what I asked. I asked what happened." He grips my hand, holding my wrist out for inspection. Every cell in my body shivers when he trails gentle fingers over my skin with all the love and care in the world. "Is this why you ran? Why you were crying?"

I can't help it. I scoff. He drops my hand and jerks back to glare at me. A giggle leaves me at the sight of him on his knees, sitting two feet below me but glaring up at me like he'd like to incinerate me or bend me over his knee. *That I can get on board with.*

He cocks a brow in question. I roll my eyes, shoving him away so I can continue to peruse the room. "No. I ran because I have no intention of watching you fuck a woman in the tank when you've spent the entire night trying to convince me to give you a chance." The words are said in a sardonic huff, but the ache in my heart remains.

He sputters. "What are you–" he breaks off.

"Did you already forget the brunette? Fuck, I guess those five minutes really weren't memorable." I bark a laugh as my fingers glide over a spanking bench. The leather is cool to the touch, even in the warm room. Now that I'm really looking around, I'm also noticing more panic buttons throughout. I assume they send the cops, or at least a heavy security protection up the take care of those situations. "Tell me, Pet. Will you forget *me* so easily?"

Despite the coolness of my tone, I know he can hear the hurt.

"Addison," he murmurs. "Look at me." I don't. He huffs. "I didn't fuck anyone." He can't see me, but I roll my eyes, even as a ball of hope blooms in my chest. "I didn't. The woman was drunk, and despite my incessant protests, she tried to pull me in. I didn't want to hurt her by physically removing her, but when I saw you run, I decided I didn't give a fuck. I shoved her away. I sent security to take care of her and let her sleep it off in a safe place."

My heart warms to new heights, and I feel the last ball of the tension drain from my body.

"I don't know what else you need me to do to prove to you that I didn't touch her, but I'll do–" Jesus. He's practically begging now. I really am a fucking bitch, aren't I?

I turn to face him, shaking my head emphatically. "I believe you, Jackson." He inhales sharply. I could, *should* apologize, but I can't bring myself to do it. I was hurt, and I had a right to be. But it's not his fault. Instead, I offer him something else. My total trust. "A man was being aggressive with me tonight and grabbed my wrist when you were with that woman." He hisses and moves to stand, probably ready to kill the guy. It makes me warm and fuzzy inside. I hold a hand up to stop him. "He didn't hurt me, Jack. Not really. I got away, and security removed him already, but then I saw you with her. That's why I ran. But I'm okay now that I'm with you."

He pauses, some of the fight leaving him, and tilts his head, observing me. His lip tips up. "You trust me." The words are like an awed praise mixed with shock.

I swallow, nodding. "I do." I wouldn't be here if I didn't. I wouldn't stay. "Don't break it."

With that, he drops down into the perfect submissive position and bows his head. I don't miss the full-blown smirk he tries to hide. "I would never dream of it, Mistress."

Turning away from him before he can see my misty eyes, I go back to my previous task. My gaze lands on the St. Andrews Cross. Something that's commonly used with female submissives, but in my opinion, there is nothing sexier than seeing a man strapped to one and helpless while a woman uses his body for her own pleasure. Takes what she wants—what she needs—forcing him to hold back until she gives him permission to let go.

The next thing I spot is a chest of drawers in the corner. I make my way to it slowly, rocking my hips as I go. Peeking over my shoulder to check on Jack, I give him a wink when I see he's still in the exact position I left him, lips dripping with saliva, slacks sitting low on his hips as he rests on his knees. His large erection is tenting his dark pants, and I take a second to let myself take in his form finally.

He's beautiful. His skin is smooth, but there's a smattering of reddish freckles across his chest that matches his nose, and it only endears him to me more. His abs are cut, as is his Adonis belt. His shoulders are broad, his muscles rippling. He's not huge or overly bulky. He's just perfect. Just Jackson.

Mine.

Okay. Calm down, Addison.

Opening the top drawer, I skim the assortment of bondage straps, Shibari ropes, chains, cuffs, zip ties, and even a roll of saran wrap. I shiver, my intense claustrophobia rearing its ugly head at the idea of mummification. Nope. Definitely too extreme. I pull out a silk blindfold and gag-ball, skipping over the bondage since the cross has chains. I drop them on the dresser and move to the second drawer.

"Scene paused," I call out, still digging through the drawer. "What are your limits, Jack? Hard and soft," I ask, realizing we haven't even had a chance to discuss this.

He answers without skipping a beat. "You can do whatever you want to me, Addy. I mean that." I shoot a shocked look at him, and he simply shrugs. "I trust you, Princess."

The nickname sends a shiver down my spine, unlike any other has before. For some reason, it hits different than your standard *baby* or *sweetheart*.

It also hit different when he called me his perfect little whore, but I digress.

"Really? Anything?" That can't be right.

Jack chuckles and rolls his eyes, clearly taking advantage of our momentary pause. "Don't shit on me."

A bark of surprised laughter escapes, and I turn to face him. Hand planted on my hip, I give him a coy smile. "But if I decide to piss on you, you'd be okay with it?" His eyes widen, and he shifts back slightly.

Gulping, he nods. "If that's what you want, I'll try it."

I shudder, turning back to the dresser. "You lucked out, handsome. I may like fluid play, but not that kind." To each their own, but personally, I draw the line at cum and spit.

"What about you?" he asks, an odd quality to his voice. I brush it off, digging through the assortment of dildos and vibrators.

"I'm claustrophobic, so no complete bondage where I can't move at all, or it would take too much to free me in an emergency." Like a panic attack, but I don't say that. "I also don't care for blindfolds or anything of the sort. And I like impact play, but I'm not into anything too harsh or painful. Pain's not my thing."

"What about the good kind of pain?" he rasps, clearing his throat. "Biting, spanking, forced orgasms?"

I shiver. Yep. I could definitely get down with that. "I consent."

"So do I," he agrees. "Safeword?" I smile to myself at his questions, grabbing my loot and spinning back toward him.

"Red is fine. You?"

He nods. "Color system. Green, yellow, red."

I smile. This is all so very—simple? Easy? I hesitate mid-step. No. Not just easy. It's *comfortable*. It feels like we've done this a hundred times. Like we're already well-versed in each other and our bodies. Like we're already...together.

Be careful, Addy. He hasn't even seen you naked yet. I tell my mother's cutting voice to fuck off, not allowing her to ruin such a pure moment.

There's a small accent table next to the cross, and I gently deposit the toys on it before looking expectantly at Jack. "Ready?"

"Are we doing this?" he asks, suddenly looking slightly hesitant.

I tilt my head to the side, taking him in. "I thought that's what you wanted?" Shit. Is he already backing out? Did he change his mind?

He nods, killing that ugly train of thought in its tracks. "Of course. I want this, Addy. I want you." He shakes his head, muttering something I can't hear but sounds a hell of a lot like, *more than anything*. "But before we start, there's something I need to do."

His eyes drift down my body, and his hand slips into his slacks, palming his cock. He groans, his hips thrusting against his hand. Shit. I want to do that. My mouth waters with the need to touch, taste, feel.

To fuck.

Meeting my gaze, he swallows hard, making his Adam's apple bob. "Permission to undress you, Mistress? I need to see you, please. I've waited a long time for this."

Panic flares momentarily, but I shove it down, using his sweet words to ground me. My walls are crumbling. My need, my want for him, outweighs everything else. My hands flex at my sides.

"Permission granted," I start. Jack immediately moves to stand, but I tut him, gaining control. "Ah, ah, ah. Earn it." He freezes. "Get naked and crawl to me, Pet, and then you can have your treat."

Chapter Thirteen

Addison

JACKSON JUMPS TO HIS feet, tearing his slacks off faster than I've ever seen anyone undress before. There is no finesse, no sensuality in his movements, yet the sight of him standing before me completely naked as he kicks his fitted boxers off is enough to have me panting.

"Perfect," I breathe, the word slipping through my lips without thought. I don't take it back, though. It's true. I meet his eyes, finding a heated expression as he stares back at me. "You're beautiful, Jackson." His real name also slips, but it feels important. This isn't a scene, it's us, and this moment is important.

"So are you, Addison," he rasps, making me shift awkwardly. Instead of letting that sink in, I scan his body in depth now that I have the chance.

He smiles a hungry, cocky smile and drops his hand down his body, gripping his solid length. My eyes follow the trail, taking in every delicious inch of him. His thighs are long and toned, covered in dark blonde hair. His hips are cut, creating a V shape that points down to his cock that he's slowly, tantalizingly stroking. I practically swallow my tongue when I realize that his one large hand hardly covers his size. He's long, thick, and curved. Perfect. He's so damn perfect.

My hands slide down my own body, settling on my stomach. Will he feel the same when he sees me? Will he hate how I look? What will—

Jackson growls and drops to his knees, crawling toward me like the perfect submissive. His cute ass sways in the air, making me chuckle and washing away some of the negative, intrusive thoughts. Stopping when he reaches me, he drops back on his haunches. His impressive cock sits proudly between his thighs, pointing directly at me. Saliva pools in my mouth as I watch a drop of precum form at his tip.

"You were a good boy for me, Jack," I whisper, letting my fingers sift through his blonde hair. It's so soft as it weaves through my fingers. It's not too long, just enough to tug, but I like the way it looks when it falls in his eyes. I jerk my chin at his cock. "Look at you. Already dripping for me." My voice is a throaty purr. He gives me a proud smirk. Licking my lip, I murmur, "Bring me a taste."

"Fuck," he breathes. He palms his cock, jerking it a few times, releasing more pre-cum. Two fingers run over the tip, collecting it for me. His hand twitches as he guides it to my lips. I shake my head.

"Tongue out, Pet." His eyes flare at my demand, but he does as I tell him. Slowly, his mouth parts, and he pokes his tongue out. I bring his hand up and glide his fingers across his flesh. "Don't move," I murmur. Leaning forward, I keep my eyes locked on his as I suck his cum coated tongue into my mouth. I moan at the flavor, causing Jack to shudder roughly. I pull off with a pop. "You taste so much better than him."

He blinks rapidly as the words sink in. He sucks in a breath when he realizes what I mean, knowing I'm referring to the cum he spit in my mouth earlier. "Thank you, Mistress."

"You're such an obedient, dirty boy for me, Pet," I praise as I straighten my spine once more. With one last shuddering breath, I nod. "You can undress me now." I know he doesn't miss the waiver in my voice.

This is different. It's different. It's different.

Jack stands. His hands reach out, gripping my hips as he drags me forward. "I'm trying, Princess, I really fucking am," he murmurs as I stumble into him. "I want to be a good boy for you. I want to show you how well I can obey your every command, but I can't sit back and watch you fill your head with this shit."

My body twitches at his words. I find his eyes and glare at him. "What are you talking about?"

His hands slide up my body, easily finding the zipper under my arm that goes down my side to my hip. He grips it slowly, ignoring the fact that I'm suddenly covered in goosebumps. "Right now," he whispers, his voice surprisingly melodic, as though he's afraid speaking any louder will cause me to bolt. He's not wrong. "You're thinking I won't love the way your body looks when I finally have the honor of seeing you bare for the first time."

His words stab me like a spear. I shiver again, harder this time. My eyes squeeze shut. The zipper drops an inch. The hand not gripping the tiny, cold metal finds its way to my throat. He collars it softly just below my choker while he continues to unzip the black dress.

"You're thinking," he begins again, "I won't find every inch of you spectacular in every—" Another inch. And another. "Single—" Two inches. "Fucking—" He reaches my hip, and the zipper ends. "Way."

Jack tightens his hold on my throat, tilting my head back. "Look at me, Addison." It takes a tremendous amount of effort, but I do. I'm shocked to find him fuzzy from unshed tears. "You're perfect." I shake my head or try to, but his grip is borderline punishing. "You. Are. Perfect." His voice is a rumbling growl. "Now drop the dress, Princess."

My brows furrow, and my hands flex. I hadn't realized I'd been holding it up. I swallow, and the ache against his fist throbs. With one deep breath, I drop the material. I couldn't wear a bra with the strapless, plunging neckline, so I already know what he'll see. My diamond choker. My tiny thong. My garter belt and straps. My knee highs. That's it. There is no tummy control. No padding. No lift or tuck. Just me.

Jack sucks in a sharp breath that has my eyes squeezing shut. I feel a cool wind tickle my skin seconds before his hand lands on my thighs. My eyes spring open, shocked to find him in a crouched position, his gaze locked on my garter straps as he works to unfasten them. I stand stock still, my mouth just as frozen as my mind, as I watch Jack slowly remove my knee-highs and garter belt. When I'm left in nothing but my tiny thong that hides absolutely nothing, he pauses. Hands on my hips, thumbs in the black lace, his eyes find mine.

"As sexy as this get-up is, I want to see all of you when I tell you that you're perfect. I want you to know without a shadow of a doubt that *I see you,* and I find you utterly intoxicating."

I shiver, fighting the urge to deny his claims. To point out my flaws. To ask why he doesn't see what I see, but it would be pointless. Body dysmorphia and severe childhood trauma. That's why my psychiatrist diagnosed me at the age of 19. That's why I know Jack doesn't see what I see and never will. All I can do is hope that one day, I'll be able to actually believe his words.

I say nothing, biting my lip to temper my breathing. Jack slowly slides my panties down my thighs, nudging my feet to step out of them. When they're gone, he stands and takes a step back. I don't know how long his eyes devour my body, but it feels like hours. Painful, embarrassing hours. I've been naked for men before. But they're trained to be quiet and do as they're told. To compliment me, thank me, beg me–yet, it means nothing when it's part of a scene. It's acting with the added benefit of pleasure. At least, that's all it's been for me. Until now.

Jack steps into me, resting his forehead against mine. In a move sweeter than any I've ever experienced before, he cradles my head, holding me to him like I'm precious. "From the first day I met you, I knew you'd bring me to my knees, and it has nothing to do with the way you look." I whimper, and his fingers trail through my ponytail. "You are the most beautiful woman I have ever seen in my life, Addison Penelope Hughes, but that beauty goes far deeper than your skin and body." He kisses my forehead softly. "You are perfection. Your monsters, broken bits and all." I nuzzle my head into his neck, wishing like hell I could force his words to penetrate my soul and rewrite its damage.

"People only see one thing when they look at me," I breathe, murmuring my biggest fear into the dark, safe space I've found myself in. "They see big boobs, a small waist, blonde hair, and long legs. They see me as a thing they can use instead of a person."

Like my mother, profiting off of my appearance, forcing me to model, even as a young child. She sexualized me and my body before I even knew what that meant. She didn't care how tired and sick I felt. She didn't care that I was deprived of vital calories and childhood experiences. She just saw the money. The clout. The beauty. It's the same thing men see when they look at me now. A hot woman meant for their pleasure, just like that man tonight.

But none of that kills me as badly as how I see myself. I think I hate the way I look so much, in part, due to the rhetoric that was spit at me from such a young age.

Work out more so you don't look fat in the photos. Don't eat that; you'll get acne. You weren't chosen for this campaign–you don't have the right look.

Eat less.

Try harder.

Lose weight.

Look at that pudge.

Ugly. Not right. Too blonde. Too tall.

The list goes on and on. It circles through my mind daily, and it's a constant battle. One I far too often lose, finding myself face down in a toilet purging my meals the way I wish I could purge my heartache. Yet, I feel that the reason I hate my body has more to do with the fact that I'd give literally anything not to look like this.

"You're more than your body, Addy," Jack says, his voice laced with vehemence. "I wish you saw what I see."

"So do I," I whisper.

Gripping my ponytail, he pulls my head back gently, dragging my eyes back to his. I momentarily protest losing my safe space. "Then I won't stop until you know how perfect you are."

I swallow thickly. "It'll take more than a night to fix a lifetime's worth of damage, Jack."

His brows lift, and an adorable smile fills his face making my heart thump erratically. "Who said we just have tonight?"

I shiver, finding his words more appealing than anything I've ever heard before. "That was what you asked for, wasn't it?"

He rolls his eyes, still grinning widely. It soothes my nerves to see him like this. Relaxed. Content. Close. To feel his body pressed against mine. It's then that I realize we're both utterly and completely naked, holding each other like it's the most natural thing in the world, and unsurprisingly, it is. I'm not thinking about his hard dick...okay, well, now I am. But before this moment, I'd just been thinking about how safe I felt wrapped up in his strong arms.

"I said you need to give me one night to prove to you that this means something, but I don't need tonight to know that." He leans in, his lips hovering over mine. "You mean more to me than anything in this world, and I swear on my life I am never letting you slip through my fingers again. I don't need a night of sex to prove that to myself; I've known it from day one."

And then, his lips crash into mine.

Chapter Fourteen

Addison

I suck in a shocked gasp at both his words and the feel of his mouth on me. This kiss–it's *the* kiss. I already know it, and it's just begun.

His fingers tangle in my hair, digging into my scalp as he controls our movements. He's demanding and forceful, but his body is soft. Guiding. Encouraging. I moan, sinking into him as my hands find his hard chest. My fingernails dig into his skin, raking against it like I'm trying to burrow my way deeper into his body until he consumes me. I want to lose myself in Jackson Lowell until I don't know where he ends and I begin.

His tongue glides across the seam of my lips, demanding entry. Entry I want to fight him for but quickly lose the battle. There are two parts of me at war when I'm with him. The part that's bold.

That dominates and demands. The one that keeps me safe and in control. The one I'm used to. Then, there's another part. A part I didn't even know I had until I met Jackson. The one that wants to give in completely, trusting that he *has* me. That he'll keep me safe while bringing me to new heights of pleasure. Pleasure I've never felt before, like earlier, at the glory hole. I trusted him to keep me safe. To take control and demand my obedience. It was hard, but when I finally gave it to him–holy shit. I've never felt pleasure like that.

Until now.

His hands slide down my body, exploring, learning. All the while, his mouth moves against mine as he devours me thoroughly. His fingers find my hard nipples. He twists and soothes before pinching roughly.

I moan loudly.

He groans and pinches harder, tugging them until they're throbbing. I bite his lip in retaliation, pulling it away from his mouth before letting go with a pop. Jack barks a laugh. "You're gonna pay for that, you little cock tease."

I giggle, unable to help myself. "In your dreams, you big baby."

He grips my breast and palms it harshly, squeezing once before soothing the hurt. His other hand comes down on my ass cheek. He slaps it once, twice, three times. I screech with each stinging blow. "You and that mouth of yours," he growls, slapping the other cheek, this time even harder.

I dig my teeth into his pec to stifle the scream and show him what my mouth is really capable of. Jack leaves my ass and wraps his fist around my ponytail, yanking it roughly, causing my back to bend. I snarl at him. "That is not a fucking leash," I snap.

He chuckles darkly, cocking a brow. "Isn't it, though?" His eyes leave mine before landing on the far wall. He smirks, bending me further until I'm looking behind me upside down. Jesus fuck. Thank God I'm flexible. "Would you prefer a real one?"

My eyes lock on an assortment of exactly that. Pet collars and leashes. My pussy throbs, and my thighs rub together awkwardly. Jack releases me enough to let me stand, never letting go of my hair. He thumbs the choker on my neck and licks his lips. His eyes dart between mine and the necklace. "I noticed this the second I saw you tonight. You know what this is, right?"

"Jewelry," I hiss, ignoring his implication.

He shakes his head, smirking. "Liar. You knew what you were doing when you wore this tonight." His jaw works, and his Adam's apple bobs. "A collar tells people you're taken. It's also for subs." His thumb trails across the thick diamond band again before slipping between it and my skin. He tugs, yanking me forward. "Tell me, *Pet*," he purrs, using my name for him. "Did you wear this to scare people off of you? To let them know you were taken and already have a master at home?"

I swallow, glancing away. I hadn't. Not at first. But then, the idea of really hooking up with someone–with allowing someone else into my heart, my world–made me sick. "No," I deny.

He barks a laugh, pulling harder. He drags my mouth back to his, and his lips ghost over me as he speaks. "But, Princess, I thought you were a Domme." I shiver at his condescending words. "Why would you want to be collared?"

I exhale roughly, deciding to just go for it. If I'm going up in flames tonight, I might as well enjoy the burn. "There is only one man I will ever allow to collar me," I whisper. My eyes meet his, and from this close, I can see the desire burning in his green orbs. "The same man who is willing to bend for me just so I can feel safe. *He* is the only man that I will ever submit to."

Jack growls. "That's fucking right, Princess, and he doesn't share."

His lips come down on down mine, and the pressure on my hair and throat is released. His hands wrap around my thighs, lifting me. My legs tangle behind his back, and my hands clench his hair. This kiss is all teeth and tongue. It's a battle of dominance. A power struggle.

My back slams against the wall. I gasp. My head drops back as I catch my breath. We're both panting. My vision is foggy. My head is dizzy. His cock is pressed against my belly. Denying me what I want, just inches from where I need him. A spike of vulnerability hits me, telling me I've done too much, said too much. I need to get control again.

I lock eyes with Jack, finding his lips red and swollen. He's panting just as hard as I am as his hips grind maddeningly against me. "Get between my thighs like a good boy, Pet. Right where I need you." I demand, running my nails down his chest and leaving red stripes behind.

Jack grunts. His hands grip my asscheeks, pulling them apart as he continues to thrust his hips against me. His mouth drops to my throat, and he bites down hard, murmuring against my skin. "Get on your knees like a good little whore, Princess. Right where you belong."

"Fuck," I cry out. His words are like gasoline on a match. I palm his cock, feeling his hot flesh for the first time. He's too big, and it takes both hands to grip him fully. God, he's going to feel incredible inside me. "Please, Jack. *Please*."

He chuckles, licking my burning flesh. "Already begging, and I haven't even touched you yet."

"Then fucking touch me," I snap.

He sucks a chunk of my skin into his mouth, leaving mark after mark along my shoulders and throat. "Such a needy little thing, aren't you?" He thrusts hard, pinning me to the wall.

"You promised," I whimper, pulling at the last threads of my sanity. "You promised we'd do this my way." He pauses, looking up at me, questions in his eyes.

"What do you need, Mistress?" he mumbles, licking his lips.

"Do you really want to know?" I ask, arching a brow.

He nods, making me smirk. *Finally*. I run my fingers over his jaw softly. "Get on your knees, Pet. Stick your tongue out and eat me from clit to ass. Don't stop. I don't want want to hear anything besides the sloppy sounds of you devouring me. I don't even want to hear you breathe. You sure you still want this?"

His eyes widen, and he groans. Jack leans in, pressing his lips to mine, this time softer. "I aim to please you, Mistress."

He carries me to the bed and drops me haphazardly on my back. I bounce, and a surprised giggle leaves my lips. Wasting no time, Jack works his way down my body, pressing sucking kisses to every inch he can find. My neck, my collar bone–paying special attention to the choker, my breasts. His palms glide up and down my ribs as his mouth does exactly what I demanded. He devours me.

My nipples are raw and aching by the time he moves further down my body. He presses soft kisses along my ribs and hip bones. A moment of insecurity hits, but before it can take root, he soothes sweet strokes over my bones with his soft fingers and dips between my thighs.

"Holy shit," I cry out. My hips arch off the bed with the first swipe of his tongue. Jack throws my legs over his shoulders and bands an arm over my hips, keeping me tethered to him.

Another lick, and he groans. "Fuck, Addy," he murmurs, causing me to shiver. My fingers find his hair, and I quickly grip it, pulling him back.

Even though I'm already shaking and on the edge, a fact I refuse to tell him, we're still doing this my way. "Try that again, Pet."

His eyes flare wide, and his cheeks pinken. "Fuck, *Mistress*," he corrects, swallowing. "You taste incredible."

I smirk. "I know. Now be a good boy and drown in my cum."

"Goddammit," he groans as his hips hump against the plush bed. "You're going to be the death of me with that mouth."

He dives back in, eating me like I'm his favorite meal. His thick tongue licks a path from my ass to clit and back again. He grips my thighs, lifting my legs higher, giving him better access to all of me.

In seconds, I'm cumming for the second time tonight. It's sharp and unexpected, barreling into me like a semi. "Jack," I cry out, tugging his hair hard, pulling him into me, refusing to let him leave, even for a second. I feel him grin against my sensitive flesh before sucking my clit into his mouth, sending another wave of sparks dancing through my body.

He drops one of my legs when my fingers loosen a fraction and pulls away enough to look up at me. "Can I trust you not to move, or do I need to strap you to the bed?"

A bark of punishment sits on my tongue, but the threat of being tied down, coupled with the evil look in his eyes, has me tucking my lips into my mouth. I nod.

"That's my beautiful slut. Thank you." My face blazes with heat, and another wave of arousal floods me at his degrading praise.

He releases his hold on me and grabs two of the pillows in the pile next to us before stuffing them under my ass to lift my hips. I expect him to settle back between my thighs, so I'm shocked when he crawls back up my body and presses a sweet kiss to my lips. "Do you like the way we taste together, Mistress?" he murmurs before shoving his tongue into my mouth. I moan, my back arching off the bed. So close. He's so close. He could just slip inside and fuck me hard, right– "Perfect, aren't we?"

I choke out a gravelly *yes*, making him chuckle before he drops back between my thighs. God, he's so good at this. I moan, fucking up my hips into his mouth. "Tell me how happy you are to be eating my pussy, Pet. Tell me how much you love it." He doesn't respond but groans loudly. In seconds, my clit's between his teeth, and two fingers are plunging deep inside me.

My hips buck up again as another orgasm builds, and just like that, he's gone. I growl, barely fighting a tantrum. "Get back down there," I snap.

He shakes his head, sighing. "I'll play your game if you'll play mine. I'll be your good little boy if you'll be my obedient slut. Stay on the bed. Do not move until I tell you to, or this all stops. Understood?"

God fucking dammit. What have I gotten myself into? Groaning, I nod.

"What's your safeword, Addison?" My eyes widen at his question. He's just eating me out, isn't he? Swallowing, I murmur *red*. "Good. Now scream for me."

Three fingers roughly plunge into my dripping pussy, curving up and finding my g-spot with unnerving accuracy. And just like he said, I scream. Again and again, Jack brings me pleasure, unlike anything I've ever known. His movements are precise. Practiced and perfected. He knows when to pause or slow down. How much more to give me. How much I can take. He adds fingers and takes them away. Sucks my clit between his teeth and bites down, only to then ignore it for countless painful minutes.

He's not just eating me out. This is a fucking religious experience.

I don't know how long it goes on, but eventually, I become delirious. I stopped counting after my twentieth orgasm. They haven't all been explosive. Some were small, tremble-inducing zaps. Some made me breathless from screaming so loud. I know for a fact I've squirted multiple times. A lot, judging by the soaking pillows beneath me. Jack never stopped, barely pausing to let me breathe. All the while, he's encouraged me, giving me words of filthy praise. He's finger fucked me within an inch of my life, yet I still feel utterly empty.

"Jack, pl-please," I stutter, vaguely aware of the fact that at some point, I've dropped the entire scene, losing control and giving it over to him. "Please," I cry...and I mean actually cry. The tears started streaming somewhere around orgasm number seven and haven't stopped since.

He pops off my clit but doesn't remove his three–or is it four–fingers from my swollen, soaked pussy. I think there might even be one in my ass. Honestly, I have no idea what's where. All I know is that everything is sensitive and throbbing with pleasure.

"What color, Addy?" he asks softly. I shake my head, black spots dancing in my vision. I don't know what to say. I'm not done. I just want *him*. "I'm here, baby." It's the love in his voice that breaks me. I didn't even realize I was talking out loud. That's how out of it I am, and yet he's still here, guiding and supporting me. A choked sob leaves my throat, but Jack doesn't move. "Say it, Addison." His opposite hand strokes my sweaty, sticky belly softly. "Tell me what you want, and it's yours."

"Ye-yellow. I need a minute, I think," I murmur, wiping my tears away. I blink rapidly to clear my vision and finally look down at him. His face is red and soaked with my releases, and the sight of it has me giggling. It's a choked, ugly sound, but it's progress. "God, I look so good all over your face."

His eyes widen, and his fingers slip from my pussy and, yes, ass, causing me to jolt. Seconds later, we're both laughing hysterically. I think I might be losing it. Jack's head drops onto my thigh, and he presses a kiss to it before dropping another to my pussy and opposite leg.

He crawls up my body, covering me in wet kisses as he goes. His hips align with mine as he drops his body on top of me. For some reason, the pressure instantly calms and soothes me. Leaning over my face with a dripping chin and dimpled smile, he kisses my nose. "What do you want, Princess?" he murmurs.

Instead of responding, I dive forward weakly and lick a path up his cheek. Jack shudders. "Such a nasty bitch, hmm?" he groans. "Licking up your cum like your starving for it."

I moan, more at his words than anything. He shifts when my heart rate finally normalizes and lifts some of his weight from my body. While he's distracted with my licks, I reach between us and grip his solid, burning cock. His hips jerk. Unable to help myself, I fist him, jacking him off slowly against my pussy. I find him already a sticky mess, making me pause. Jack chuckles an adorable sound. "I couldn't help myself. I think I made more of a mess on the bed than you did."

"You came?" I ask, slightly shocked. "From eating me out?"

He licks my tear-stained cheeks in a move that feels incredibly possessive and animalistic. "Can you blame me?"

I snicker, rolling my eyes as I continue to slowly pump his cock. "Let me guess," I murmur, rubbing his length against my dripping pussy. He hits my clit, and my hips thrust up into him, causing us both to groan. "I taste like the best meal you've ever had?"

He exhales, leaning to brace himself on his forearms over my body, keeping us face to face. We're still sprawled out in the center of the massive bed, sideways and horizontal with the pillows, covered in sticky fluids. But judging by the way he's making himself comfy, we're both content to stay here.

Shaking his head, he locks eyes with me, shifting his hips in my grip, causing me to release him. I feel him hover just outside of my opening. Neither of us moves an inch, feeling like we're standing on the edge of something else. Something more.

Everything.

"No, Princess," he murmurs, dropping his lips to mine and hovering just like he is with his cock. "You taste like forever."

And then, he fucks into me in one brutal thrust.

Chapter Fifteen

"**F**uck," she cries out at the same moment I release a shuddering groan.

Fuck is right. She feels so good. Tight. Hot. Dripping. It takes everything inside of me not to pull back out and fuck into her ruthlessly. Instead, I drop my head into the crook of her neck. I breathe in her sweet, sweaty scent while we both get used to the feeling of my cock buried deep inside of her.

Her pussy flutters around me, and I groan again, my hips bucking against hers. "Goddammit, Addy," I choke out. "Hold the fuck still for a second, or I'm gonna blow my load already."

"You can, you know," she whispers. The nerves in her voice have me arching back to meet her eyes. My brows dip at her bashful look. She glances away, biting her lip. I give a small teasing thrust, and her eyes snap back to me. I cock a brow, waiting her out. She rolls her eyes. Shit. I can't wait to fuck that attitude out of her someday. I scoff internally. Yeah, right. I love her attitude. "You can cum inside me," she whispers.

It takes me a second for her words to penetrate through the haze of lust. The tiny thread of control I'd been clinging to *snaps*. My hips bull back, and I slam into her before I've even realized what I've done. I know she's on birth control since I read her application, and having a clean STD panel was required for entry to the party, but hearing her say I can cum inside of her sweet pussy does something to me. It releases the feral beast that wants to rut. To claim. To breed.

Mine. Addison is mine.

Fuck. I really need to stop reading Shiloh's books.

Except now that the thought has sunk in, it won't leave. I want to knock her up. Keep her tied to me. More than that, I just plain want her. Forever.

I tune back into Addy, finding her head tipped back, face blissed out in pleasure, as she's forced to submit to my punishing thrusts. Shit. I didn't even realize I was fucking her so hard. I can't stop. I don't want to. She feels too perfect–too mine. But this is our first time, and I'd fucking kill myself if I screwed things up for us by taking this too far.

I pause my brutal thrusts, panting to catch my breath. I grip her jaw, silencing her protest. Making sure she's paying attention, I ask, "Do you want to be my Princess or my pretty little slut right now? You decide how this goes."

She sucks in a breath. Her icy blue eyes are hooded with lust, and her chest is rising and falling, causing her juicy tits to bob in a tantalizing rhythm. She swallows and tips her chin up. "Fuck you, Jackson." My mouth drops open in shock, but my cock twitches inside of her. Her lip lifts, and I realize what she's just done.

Fuck. Fuck. Fuck.

"What's your safeword, slut?" I growl.

She smirks. "Red, asshole."

I grip her chin harder and press my mouth to hers in a punishing, dangerous kiss. She bites my lip hard, drawing blood. Leaning back, I glare at her, feeling everything in my body scream, *be careful with this one. She's precious.* And she is. But she's also being a fucking brat, and she's playing dirty. My hand tips back before I bring it down on her cheek. The slap is a warning, a punishment. It's not hard enough to injure, but it gets the point across. It also has her moaning and clenching around my cock. I chuckle, pushing back to sit on my knees. My hips buck hard, again and again.

"Fuck, you really are a nasty slut, hmm?" I groan, feeling my balls already tightening as lightning dances down my spine.

"God, yes," she cries as her fingers scramble for purchase on the comforter. "More, Jack. *Harder.*"

I slap her thigh, devouring the sound of her gasping moan. "You don't need harder. You need deeper." I lean back, gripping her ankles and shoving her legs up and open, spreading her wide for me so I can get as deep as possible.

"Holy shit," she screams, making me grin. I tip my hips to reach a different angle. One I know will blow her mind. "Yes, Jackson. Yes, fuck."

"You like being my greedy, cock hungry brat, don't you?" I bark, snapping my hips forward hard enough to bruise her cervix. Maybe if I fuck her deep enough, I'll slip inside it. "You like feeling me so deep inside of you that you'll never be able to get me out of your system?" I pull back, pausing for her answer. She nods, her head bobbing sloppily. I snap forward again. "So deep you'll never get rid of me. Never not know what it feels like to be owned by my cock."

Her head shakes back and forth as she cries and whimpers. She's so close she doesn't know what to do with herself. I shove her right leg and slap her thigh again. "Keep this here." I release her and wait to see if she does as I said. Her leg wobbles in exhaustion, but she keeps herself spread open for me with the help of her hand. "That's my filthy slut. So hungry for it, you'd do anything I tell you to, wouldn't you?"

"Yes, Sir," she whimpers, causing precum to shoot from my balls.

My thumb finds her clit as I reward her perfect behavior and listening skills. My eyes drop down, taking in the sight of my big cock disappearing inside of her. She's so wet; she's dripping down my shaft and making a wet spot beneath us, adding to her previous releases. I grunt, biting my lip. I can't look away. She's perfect. She was made for me.

"You look so good taking my cock," I praise breathlessly, rubbing her clit harder. She cries out, shaking as her orgasm barrels into her. It's her twenty-second of the night, so I can assume it's painful. "Cry harder, Addison. Scream so loud they can hear you through the soundproofed walls."

Her wild, frantic eyes find mine as her body trembles. She releases the bedspread and reaches one delicate hand out to me, and I swear to God, everything inside of me shifts. She's reaching *for me*. Needing me closer. My hips pause as I take in the vulnerable expression on her face, and I know–I just know–she's finally letting me in. I bat her hand away, not missing the hurt in her eyes. I don't want to hold her hand, though. I want to hold *her*.

"I've got you, Princess," I murmur, wrapping my arms under her small body. My cock stays deep inside of her as I lift her up, settling her on my bent thighs. Her chest presses against mine, and her hands weave in my hair, something I've noticed she loves doing.

Addy gasps at the new angle, feeling my cock so deep inside of her she can barely move. "That was incredible," she whispers, looking surprisingly bashful. "I've never cum so many times or so hard in my life."

I chuckle, pressing a kiss to her forehead. "We aren't done yet," I say with a thrust of my hips. She moans. With one arm banded behind her back, I keep her safe and steady on my lap. With the other, I fist her messy ponytail, arching her back and giving me access to her glorious tits. "Say thank you for the orgasms, Sir," I murmur against a nipple, smoothing my hand up and down her back. "And ride me till' I cum deep inside your pretty pussy."

Addison moans. "Fuck." I slap her ass hard. She sucks in a breath. "Th-thank you for the orgasms, Sir," she mumbles, her voice raspy from overuse. Her hips rock in small movements that have my eyes going spotty. With every sensual grind, her clit hits my pelvis, causing her walls to clench. My mouth devours her breasts and nipples–biting and sucking like I'll never see them again.

Slowly, she works herself over me, moaning and whimpering, creating the best soundtrack I've ever heard. I'd been on edge for her all damn night. My balls were aching by the time we made it in this room, and the second she demanded I eat her pussy and ass, I knew I was a ticking time bomb. I came twice while fucking her with my mouth and hand. I couldn't help it. Hearing her screaming moans, feeling her tighten and drip, coating my face in her cum–it was too much to take. Now, here I am, not even an hour later, ready to fill her warm pussy with so much cum, she'll be dripping for days. It's just Addy. I've waited years for this woman. Years. *You'll have her forever, though.* The thought has me releasing her hair and back, shifting to grip her hips and instantly fucking up into her.

Addison's hands dig into my shoulders, and her eyes meet mine. I lift her up and drop her back down, using her for my pleasure. I'm done denying myself and holding out. She bites her lip and shakes as she grips me with her cunt. "Need to fill you up, Addy," I breathe, voicing a thought I've never said out loud in my entire life. Her eyes widen momentarily before she nods. I shake my head. "You don't understand. I need you dripping with my cum. I need you dripping with *me*."

"Yes," she nods again. "Fill me up. Use me like the dirty whore I am." Her words do it for me. She doesn't understand my meaning, but she will. Either way, she'll get what she wants. I groan, lifting her and dropping her up and down in frantic movements, jacking myself off with her hot pussy.

I slam her down hard as my balls draw up, and electricity shoots through me. I hold her in a bruising grip, nearly dying when she cums with me. My head drops onto her chest as I bellow her name. My entire body is trembling, and my heart is soaring. Jet after jet of cum fills her sweet pussy. She wrings me for everything I'm worth, like she's trying to drain my body.

"Jackson," she whimpers. I pull away from her plush chest and meet her eyes. They're misty, but it's not the same anxious look I'd seen before. It's so much more than that.

Exhaling roughly, I gather her to me, holding on for dear life. "I know, baby. I know."

I don't know how long we sit there, but it's long enough that the sound of Addison's loudly growling stomach and the feeling of my legs cramping pulls me away from her. My cock has mostly softened as it rests inside her body. We're both a sticky mess. Addy is flushed and limp in my arms. I lean back, finding her hazy eyes.

"When was the last time you ate, Princess?" I murmur. Her body tenses, and she looks down at the space between us. I grip her chin softly but firmly, making her look at me. "When, Addison?"

She tilts her shoulder, swallowing thickly. "Before I came." I cock a brow, not believing her one bit. Especially when it growls again. "Yesterday–" I barely stifle a growl. "Morning."

I suck in a sharp breath, squeezing my eyes shut. I try–I really try–not to yell or freak out. I know that's not the approach she needs. I also know this will be a lifelong journey for us. Us, because that's what she has now. A partner. A best friend. A protector. "Can you tell me why, baby?"

"I like Princess," she mutters offhandedly, making me smirk. She rolls her eyes and brings her hands between us. Tracing shapes across my chest that have me shivering and my stupid cock perking up, she sighs. "I didn't want to look fat in my dress today."

This time, I do growl. Rolling my neck, I collar her throat and drag her face to mine. "You could gain a hundred pounds and still be stunning." She tries to shake her head, but I don't let her. "I know this will not happen overnight. I know it will take a long time for you to believe me. Even longer for you to see what I see, but trust me when I tell you this–" I pause, waiting for her eye contact.

"You are no longer in this alone. Do you understand me? You have me now. When you're scared or vulnerable. When you're questioning yourself. Judging yourself." Swallowing, my hands flex on her skin. "Or hurting yourself... I'll be there. When the voices in your head tell you hurtful things, you have me. I'll remind you how incredible you are. I'll prove to you that I love you despite the ugly lies they whisper. You don't have to be alone any longer, Addison. Not if you don't want to be."

She's crying now, but we're both ignoring it. This is hard for her. I get it, but I also meant what I said.

It takes her a few minutes to respond, and when she does, all she can mutter is, *thank you*. I leave it as is for now, knowing it's the best

I'll get when she's overwhelmed. She moves to crawl off of me, but I stop her. "One more thing," I murmur, gripping her hips hard. "The next time I hear you say bullshit about not eating or find out that you're depriving yourself of the nutrients your body needs, I will bend you over my knee and redden your ass until you get the message. You got me?"

Swallowing, she nods.

I smile, press a kiss to her shocked lips, and lift her off me so I can get up. "Stay here for a minute," I murmur, depositing her limp body on the pillows at the head of the bed. Standing up, I groan when my knees nearly buckle. *Fuck.* Being 36 is hard.

Swiping my hand down the blacked-out service screen to wake it up, I quickly order a massive meal, likely meant for twenty people, and call for room service to change the sheets and pillows. I also order someone to come into the attached room and take care of the request I made earlier. They give me a 30-minute estimate on everything, so I head to the en-suite and fill up the huge soaker tub, adding chocolate-scented bubbles and strawberry oils. I turn the lights down low and click on the surround sound, switching the playlist to the one I created for tonight.

Like I said, I thought of everything because she deserves everything.

Lastly, I flick the lock on the second door in the bathroom that leads to the adjoining room since staff will pop in there to set it up. I don't want to risk anyone walking in on my woman naked. When the tub's full and I've taken a two-minute long piss, I head back to get Addy. She's half asleep and adorably spread out in the middle of the bed.

I pause and take a minute to soak her in. She's still wearing the collar but nothing else. Visions of her truly collared for me, fill my mind, making my tired cock pulse. My eyes scan down her body, seeing the remnants of our sex-athon. One that I've no doubt is nowhere near done. Her legs are spread slightly, giving me a view of her swollen, red pussy. *Shit*. Maybe we are done for a while.

But then I see my cum dripping from her, and my cock decides he's firmly against the plan to wait.

"Are you just going to stare at me?" she murmurs, her voice sleepy and weak. I chuckle, bending to scoop her up. She giggles and drops her head into my neck. Her fingers weave through my hair, and I can't help but kiss her forehead. "Nope," I say, popping the p. "I'm going to take care of you."

Her head pops up as we pass the St. Andrews cross on the way to the bathroom, and she pouts, pointing a limp finger at it. "I had plans for that."

Chuckling, I smack her ass lightly as I step into the steaming, deep tub. "We've got all weekend for your plans, Princess."

She gasps as her skin hits the water and clings to me. I settle us down, keeping her cradled to my chest. "All weekend?" she murmurs sleepily.

Cupping water in my palm, I bring it up to cover her shoulders, warming her up. "Yes," I murmur. "I booked the room for us until Sunday." Which gives us two days to enjoy each other in all ways. "How are you feeling?" I murmur.

Settling deeper into me, she cuddles herself into my chest, melting my heart and causing my cock to pulse all in one go. "Perfect," she murmurs. Her stomach disagrees, and I wait for her to say something. When she doesn't, I pinch her outer thigh. She groans, pulling away from me. "Tired, satisfied, and starving. Are you happy?"

I smile, shifting her to sit between my thighs so I can take care of her. "Immensely. Thank you." She nods, leaning against my chest. I reach up, gently pulling the rubberband from her hair. She shivers and quietly asks what I'm doing. "Taking care of my woman," I say simply. "Tip your head back for me, Princess."

Addison pauses, and though her back's to me, I swear I hear a muffled sob. My heart clenches. I don't think anyone has ever taken care of her after sex. I help her dip her hair into the water, happy when I see the tub is big enough for her body to still be fully submerged while I soak her hair. Her eyes drift closed, and she releases a sleepy, content sigh. The sound of *Say You Won't Let Go by James Author* plays softly through the speakers. Addy smiles softly as I pull her back into me so I can lather her hair.

"I love this song," she whispers.

Massaging shampoo through her long strands, I grin proudly behind her back. "I know." She says nothing but moans softly as I scrub her scalp. By the time the next three songs have played, I've washed her hair twice, making sure to thoroughly clean her thick mass of locks, and conditioned it once. The fourth song comes on, and though I know she's sensed a theme, she hasn't said anything yet.

I'll Be by Edwin McCain comes on, and finally, she breaks the otherwise silence. "These are love songs," she chokes out, gripping my knees. "My favorite love songs."

Tugging her against me by her hair, I wait until she's looking up at me. "I know," I murmur again. I run my hand down her cheek. "Maybe we can play it at our wedding one day."

She grins, rolling her eyes, likely thinking I'm kidding. I'm not. I'm gone for this girl. "You have to stop saying things like that, Jack," she sighs, letting her hands sway through the water.

"No," I say simply.

She turns a vaguely irritated look in my direction and scowls at whatever she finds on my face. "Why not?"

I shrug, coating the washrag in strawberry-scented soap. "Because I won't lie to you." She bites her lip and continues to play with the water. "Come here," I beckon her back into my reach and then tug her by the hand when she ignores me.

I run the soapy cloth over her skin, making sure to remove all the sweat and sticky fluids from earlier so she can feel fresh while we eat. When I've just finished her back and am heading toward her legs, she finally looks up at me. "Why are you doing all of this?" I pause, arching a brow in confusion. She waves her hand around the bathroom, the tub.

"Washing you?" I ask. She nods, then shakes her head, then shrugs. I chuckle, dipping the cloth between her legs. She moans, arching back when I start to softly wash her abused pussy.

"Have you ever entered a sub-space, Addy?" She thinks about it for a moment before shaking her head. "Do you think you did tonight?" She nods immediately. I smile. "Whether we fuck hard and fast, or I make love to you for hours, I will always take care of you." I pause, not really wanting to ask this question but needing to. "Do you take care of your subs when you're done?"

She gives me a surprised, incredulous look. "Of course. Aftercare is just as important as sex, if not more."

I nod, figuring that's what her answer would be. "But who takes care of you?" This time, she wilts in my hands. I knew it. "I do," I cut in before she can retreat in on herself. "From now on, I do. No matter what we do or who's involved. Whether it looks like what we did with that man earlier or it's just us in our bed. I will take care of you, Addison. You just need to let me."

She stares at me for a long moment before leaning forward, closing the small space between us. Her fingers thread through my hair, and she presses her lips to mine before pulling away and smiling down at me. She's crawled into my lap and positioned herself over my cock but is making no move to slide down my shaft.

"And I'll take care of you," she murmurs. "Starting now." Tugging me forward, she grins. "Dip down so I can wash your hair." And she does.

Wordlessly, she takes care of me exactly how I did her, and I let her. She needs to know that trust goes both ways. When we're done, and I'm sure she's come back down to her baseline, if not still sleepy and hungry, I pick her up and bundle her in a towel. I work another through her hair, catching as much of the water as I possibly can before tossing it into the dirty bin. She grabs another plush towel and dries my body before wrapping it around my hips.

Smiling, I bend down, palm her cheeks and kiss her hard. She sinks into me with a moan. God, I love this woman.

I pull away, leaving her dreamy and dazed. Before she knows what's happening, I lift her up bridal style, loving the way she screeches and hooks her arms around my neck. "Grab that for me," I murmur, jutting my chin toward a hairbrush and bottle of lotion on the vanity. She grins, scooping them up. Turning toward the door she hasn't been through yet, I unlock it and carefully maneuver her so I can open it.

"Where are we going?" I don't answer until we're through, and I hear her quiet gasp.

Smiling, I look down at her stunning blue eyes and nearly melt when I see them teary. "Happy Valentines Day, Princess."

Chapter Sixteen

Addison

THE ROOM IS SMALL and cozy, almost completely the opposite of the room where we had sex. The walls are a warm navy blue. Instead of cement floors, this room has dark wooden slats with plush, fur throw rugs all over the place. A large wooden framed fireplace sits in the center of the wall directly across from the doorway, with a flatscreen TV mounted above. There's a massive, sable-colored leather couch positioned in front of it. To the right, there's a giant basket that's overflowing with warm, fuzzy blankets. Next to it sits two white furry bean bags, creating the perfect spot to nestle and relax. Maybe read one of the hundreds of books filling the shelves that line the wall on either side of the fireplace. On the left side wall is a small table and mini fridge that looks stocked full of drinks and snacks.

It's warm, rustic, and beautiful, but it's not what has my eyes filled with tears and my heart beating erratically.

No. That's 100% due to the fact that the beautiful space is *covered* in candles and vases of roses. There's a full display of fancy food spread out on the table and end tables bracketing the couch. Roses take up empty corners in the room, over the mantle, the floor. There's even a vase on the mini-fridge. My eyes land on a massive heart-shaped box of Valentine's chocolates that says *You're Perfect The Way You Are* scrawled on top. For some reason, it's the sight of it that sets me off.

Big, choking sobs pour from my soul as I cling to Jackson. No one, and I mean no one, has ever done something for me like this. I've never celebrated Valentine's Day, nor have I had a Valentine before. All of that pales in comparison to the fact that no one has ever *cared* for me like this.

"Hey," he murmurs, stepping into the room and kicking the door shut. He makes his way to the couch, which of course, is covered in more plushy blankets. This really is the perfect room, and the second he drops on the couch in front of the warm, electric fireplace, I find myself melting, tears and all. "Hey, none of that, Addy. It's okay. If it's too much, just tell me, and we can go back to the playroom."

I shake my head, sniffling and sucking in an embarrassing amount of snot. I turn, straddling his thighs, and grip his face. I'm ruining the sweetest surprise I've ever been given. "No, it's not that. This is all so perfect. I'm just–" I release a shuddering breath, searching for the right words. I tip my shoulder, finally settling for, "I'm happy."

He blinks a few times, seeming to shake himself out of his panic, and smiles. I lean in and kiss him, immediately sinking into the feel of his body against mine. I reach up to tug my towel away, but he pulls back and shakes his head. "No, baby," he murmurs breathlessly. "I need to feed you, and you need to stay covered." I cringe at his words, my mind racing with ugly, vile thoughts. "Not like that," he says abruptly, squeezing my jaw. "I need you to stay covered because if I see you naked right now, I'll say fuck the food and be balls deep in your pretty little mouth before either of us knows what's happening."

Swallowing, I nod as relief fills me, then chuckle when his words really sink in. I roll my eyes, scoffing as I climb off his lap. "Sounds like you have control issues, Mr. Lowell." I stand, stepping away from him. "You might wanna work on that." With a wink, I turn to the food.

He jumps up, reaching to grab me with a growl. Screeching, I duck out of his grasp and clamber over the couch arm, avoiding him.

"Be careful," he warns, eyeing the candles. I lean back against the soft leather, panting as my eyes trail over the room again, taking in the many, *many* flames.

A burst of laughter barrels out of me. "This is a massive lawsuit waiting to happen."

Jack freezes and rears back before barking a loud laugh and nodding. "Yeah, you're right about that. Flames, flowers, and fucking don't mix."

"Especially where drunk people and orgies are concerned." He arches a brow while piling heaps of food onto a plate. I grab a blanket and tuck it around my body, sinking into the couch.

"Orgies?" I nod, accepting the plate and bottle of water he passes me. "Didn't you see them earlier?" He gives me a wide-eyed look before settling down in the opposite corner with his own plate and drink. His legs kick out, tangling with mine, and I give a happy sigh as I continue. "There were a few groups of four or five people playing in the scenes, and one of them left to the suites together."

"Five?" he asks before chuckling and shaking his head. He bites into a piece of bruschetta and eyes me warily. "Eat, Princess."

Swallowing, I look down at my plate and mentally begin to calculate calories. Everything is heavy, processed, and fatty. I settle for a grape and pop it into my mouth, forcing myself not to think about how I look eating in front of Jackson.

"Five is too many," he says offhandedly, distracting me. "I draw the line at four. Anything more than that sounds like chaos in the bedroom." I nod, digging into a chunk of what I believe is goat cheese. I moan, my eyes fluttering at the milky, sharp taste.

"I agree," I say once I've swallowed. A thought occurs to me, and I cock my head, meeting his gaze. "Have you ever shared more than one partner?"

He bites into an olive stack on a toothpick that looks delicious, and I wiggle my toes happily when I find two of them on my plate. "I have," he says gently like he's worried I'll freak out.

I roll my eyes. "I don't mind hearing about your sexual encounters, Jack. I'm not naive enough to believe you were a virgin before tonight, and I know what you like. You're a bisexual pleasure dom, and judging by your performance a little while ago, you have tons of experience."

He chokes on a piece of meat, and a burst of laughter falls from his sweet lips. "A ton, huh?"

I nod, working my way mindlessly through the snacks. I really was starving, and we just worked up one hell of an appetite. "To answer your question, yes. I've been with men and women, both together and separately. The most I've been with at once was two other men and one woman."

Lust pools low in my belly as well as a small tendril of jealousy. It's not over him being with other people, per se. Maybe just the idea that they, or someone else, can give him something I can't. I know that's a backward way of thinking. No single person can fill all of your gaps and slot into you like a perfect puzzle piece. It doesn't work that way. No one can be your everything. We're all broken and fractured, and sometimes, it takes multiple pieces to complete your puzzle.

But the insecure demons in my mind are now whispering that I won't fit into *any* of Jack's pieces, and that thought hurts a surprising amount.

"Addison," he murmurs, tapping me with his foot. "Where did you go?"

I blink, finding him staring at me with a concerned gaze. His plate is gone, and he's swapped his empty water for a flute of champagne. I blink again, looking down at my own plate, shocked to find it completely empty. It was a big plate. And…I ate it all. My eyes burn, and my stomach twists. Bile works its way up my throat, and I quickly toss the plate onto the table as if to rid myself of the evidence.

"Why didn't you say something?" I snap, fear and embarrassment replacing all other thoughts. Jack sets his glass down and leans forward, observing me. I hate it.

"Say something about what?" he murmurs softly like he's approaching a wild animal.

"Tell me to stop eating," flies out of my mouth before I can hold it back.

His eyes widen, but this time, in anger. "And why the fuck would I tell you to do that?" he barks. I rise, shaking my hands out frantically as anxiety builds. My eyes snap to the bathroom, and my feet beg to move, but Jackson is here, and I… "Why, Addison?"

My hand lands on my belly, and before I know what I'm saying, the words tumble out. "Because that was too much, Jack. I can't–I don't eat that much. *Ever*. I'll gain too much weight. I'll get fat." I scoff, running a hand through my hair that's dried in tangles while we were talking. *And eating.*

"So what?" he snaps, shoving to his feet. "Get fat. Or don't. I don't care either way, as long as you're healthy."

I roll my eyes and shoot him a disbelieving look.

No one likes a big woman my mother used to say. Again and again. *No one will want you.*

"I thought you said you wouldn't lie to me, Jackson. You'd care if I changed. If I gained any more weight. You'd care." I don't know who I'm trying to prove it to, him or me.

Jack stares at me, his face red and pinched. His hands are fisted at his sides. The look on his face has my mouth snapping shut and my feet freezing. Then, he's charging forward and throwing me over his shoulder. I cry out, scrambling for purchase as he thunders through the small, cozy room toward the bathroom. He continues through until we reach what he referred to as the playroom. Suddenly, the world is turning again as he drops down onto the edge of the bed and shifts me, so I'm laying over his knees, ass up.

"What the fuck are you d–" I don't get to finish as my towel is unceremoniously tugged away from my body, and my ass is put on full display. Seconds later, his hand is coming down on my cheeks. One after another after another. "Jackson," I cry out, slapping whatever part of his legs I can reach.

"You will *never* say that shit to me again, Addison," he barks as he continues to rain down, burning slaps over my ass and thighs. "Never again will I hear you talk so poorly about yourself." *Slap.* "Never again will I hear you put yourself down like that." *Slap. Slap. Slap.* "Never again will I watch you purposefully deprive yourself." *Slap. Slap. Slap.*

The hits burn, but they aren't aggressive in a way that has me concerned for my safety. I know he's trying to teach me a lesson.

I know he's angry. I just don't know why he cares so goddamned much. *Yes, you do.* I swallow, batting away my tears. I do. I know I do.

"Never again, Addison." He soothes my stinging asscheeks in apology as his words quiet from their previous bark. "I need you to be healthy and safe and looked after. Do you understand me?"

I sniffle and nod, then think better of it when my head swims from being upside down. "Yes, Sir," I whimper. "I'm sorry."

He sighs and presses a kiss to my backside. "I know, Princess. I know this will take time, but fuck, Addy. Seeing you like that–" I feel him shudder as he exhales. "Seeing you so mad at yourself for fueling your precious body, baby, I can't watch that. You need to try for me, Addy."

I suck in a breath and squeeze his calf. "I'll try." That's the best I can give him. I've been in therapy for years, and though I rarely binge and purge anymore, it still happens. I know for a fact if Jack hadn't been here tonight, I would have.

His hand comes down on my cheek again, and I groan. "I thought you already punished me?" I murmur, swallowing thickly as the burn turns into something else.

He chuckles, groping my flaming cheek. "Oh, I did. This is for me." He spanks me again before dipping his fingers between my thighs. My hips buck when he slips one finger right inside of me. "And you," he murmurs.

His finger pumps in and out of my sensitive core at a maddeningly slow pace. My body breaks out in shivers. He lifts his hand from my lower back where he'd been holding me down and palms my ass, all the while that one finger moves in and out, in and out. It's a tease. A taste. And not nearly enough.

I feel him shift before I hear the telltale sound of him spitting. I moan when his warm saliva drips between my cheeks, coating my asshole. "I'm going to play with you, Princess, and then I'm going to fuck you." I moan again, his words igniting me deep down to my core.

"Are you going to fuck my ass, Sir?" I purr, pressing my butt into his palm.

He grunts, gripping my cheek harshly to still me. "Is that what you want?" he murmurs.

I nod, whimpering when he presses two fingers into my pussy and works one into my ass. "Yes, please, Sir. I want you to fill me up."

Jackson growls. "I don't think you understand my obsession with filling you, Addison. I don't think that's something you're ready to fully comprehend yet." I shudder at his words.

I meant I wanted him to fill me up with his cock, but now that he's talking about his cum again, I can't shake the thought. When he came inside me earlier, it bought on a blinding orgasm. I've done a lot, but I've never fucked unprotected. I've never felt warm cum inside me like that. It feels dirty and taboo which is saying something considering all the shit I've done.

He pumps in and out slowly, occasionally spitting to add more lube so he can slip another finger in my ass. When he's confident that I'm prepped and stretched out, he kisses my spine and slips from my ass. Gently, he lifts me from his body and drops me on the bed.

"Hands and knees, slut." I quickly scramble to get into position, making him chuckle. His palm collides with my sensitive ass. This time, it's more of a love tap. "Face in the sheets. Don't move. Don't look up. Just trust me."

I shiver and nod. My eyes squeeze shut as I bury my face in the bed and shove my ass out, spreading my thighs wide. I hear the sink in the bathroom running, and I assume he's washing his hands, which I appreciate greatly. The sound of him rummaging through the chest of drawers has my spine tingling and my belly fluttering with excitement.

Minutes later, the bed dips behind me. I hear the click of a lube bottle, and I nearly groan. "Are you ready, Princess?" he murmurs as his hands smooth gently down my spine.

"Slut," I murmur, shivering again. "I'm your slut, Sir."

He chuckles, palming my asscheek roughly before slapping it twice. "Yes, you fucking are, aren't you." It's a statement. One he sounds incredibly smug about, but I'm too excited to care. Cool lube coats my asshole seconds before I feel the blunt tip of his condom covered cock press against my entrance. "Bare down for me, or I'll force my way in," he growls.

I do as he says, even though I'm not scared of his threat. He hedges forward, entering me easily with a pop.

Jackson grunts, gripping my hips. "That's it, slut. Take my cock like the dirty little whore you are." I moan, pressing back, taking him quickly down to the base of his shaft.

He shouts, probably not expecting I'd be so eager. When he's fully sheathed, I feel something else press against the tight ring of muscle that makes me pause. Jack squeezes my hips and slips out, making the both of us cry out. When just the thick tip of him is left, he pauses. "What's your safeword, Addison?"

We both know I know it, but that's his way of warning me that things are about to get heavy and that I'm still safe. More than that, I'm adored. "Red."

He rubs my spine again. "Good girl," he murmurs.

Suddenly, I feel something press against the entrance of my pussy. I suck in a breath, realizing both of his hands are on my hips, and his cock is in my ass. "What is that?" I ask, but it comes out a heavy moan when he leans forward, rolling his hips into me. In seconds, I've gone from being full of one cock, to being stuffed with two. "Jack," I scream. My entire body lights up, feeling like I've touched a live wire. "Jack," I pant, unable to find any other words to say.

"How do you feel?" he asks, his voice raspier than before, like he's fighting his need to fuck me brutally. "Are you okay?"

I nod, already on the verge of sobbing. "So good."

He groans and huffs out a laugh. "You're about to get so much better, slut."

That's the only warning I get before he adds vibration into the mix and thrusts in fully. The vibration hits my clit in this position, and I scream so loud I have to bury my face in the blankets. Jack pulls out and thrusts back in. This time, he angles his hips to hit me deeper, allowing the dildo in my pussy to glide over my g-spot.

"It's a strap-on made for double penetration," he grunts, gripping my hips to fuck up into me at a mind-blowing page. "And it feels fucking incredible. I feel like I'm sharing your perfect body with another man, Addy. Can you picture it?"

My ass and pussy flutter as my orgasm nears at his words, and Jack barks a curse in response. He slows his thrusts. Then suddenly, he stops completely. I cry out, aching for more. Needing to finish. His hand collides with my outer asscheek. "Bring your ass back on my dick. Fuck yourselves on my cocks."

I moan, pushing up to my hands and knees so I can obey him. In no time, I've found a rhythm that has me careening toward the edge once more. He spanks me again and again as he sits on his knees, letting me ride him as though he's a king on a throne. "You're such a greedy little slut, aren't you?" He groans, squeezing my sore ass. "My greedy little slut. Look at you, fucking yourself like you're starving for it."

I shudder, unable to hold back. I feel fuller than I've ever felt before, and the pleasure is otherworldly. "I'm gonna cum, Jackson," I cry out, shoving back and bracing for what I know is going to be an earth-shattering climax.

And then, he's gone.

I scream, beating the bed as I prepare to throw a full-blown tantrum. How dare he take that away from me? "No, no, no," I sob.

Before I can really fall apart, Jack returns. It's probably only been seconds but it felt like hours. "You don't cum unless it's around my cock, and you're dragging me into ecstasy with you," he growls, shoving his bare cock into my pussy. I can tell the condom and toys are gone.

Now it's just him and me.

He pushes me down onto my stomach and drives into me hard with a ferocious growl. His palms slam down on the bed next to my face, and I tilt to the side to find his eyes. Like this, flat with my legs shoved together, his knees bracketing my thighs, my pussy feels full to bursting, and I hardly miss the previous pressure from the double penetration.

My pussy flutters, and Jack growls again. He shifts, bundling my messy hair up and tugging it to the side. We lock eyes as he rolls his hips. "That's it," he whispers. "You're taking me so well, beautiful. You were made for my cock." I don't know what comes over me, but for the first time in my life, I believe Jackson Lowell with every fiber of my being. I was made for him.

"Make a mess on me so I can make one inside you," he coaxes.

"Jack," I breathe as my spine tingles, and everything inside of me coils, ready to snap.

He shakes his head, pulling my hair slightly. "I'm fucked up over you, Addison. I'm so goddamned obsessed that you've got me thinking crazy shit." His hips roll again and again. Every time he slides in deeper. His pelvis hits my aching ass, and the burning sensation only drags me higher. "You've got me thinking about filling this tiny pussy up so full of my cum, you'll be knocked up before I pull out. Birth control be damned."

I whimper, and he fucks into me harder. My pussy pulses. His words are doing things to me, and shit, I must be as fucked up as him because somewhere deep inside, I want that too.

"Gonna knock you up and keep you tied to me for the rest of your life. Do you get me?" I nod, knowing it's crazy talk but loving it just the same. "Now fucking cum, slut."

I do.

Immediately and loudly.

I cum so hard I'm pretty sure I black out. When I blink back to reality, Jack is groaning into my hair and pumping his hips in rough twitches.

"Fuck, Addy," he breathes. "*Fuck, fuck, fuck.*"

"Jack," I whisper.

"So good. So perfect. *Mine.*" I shudder. He tugs my hair gently until I blink up at him. "Say it," he murmurs, swallowing. "Say you're mine." My heart thumps for a whole new reason, but I can't find a single thing to say other than the one word rolling around on my tongue.

"Yours."

He grins and presses his lips to mine. The angle is awkward, and my pussy is dripping onto the sheets, but I don't care. We kiss slowly, softly, until our breath evens and our bodies relax. His hips roll once, twice, making us both groan.

"What are you doing?" I giggle.

Jack drops his head into the crook of my neck and lets out a confused, annoyed groan. "Making sure my cum has a chance to get where it needs to go." I wait for him to say he's kidding, but he doesn't, and it only makes me laugh that much louder.

"Jackson," I choke out between chuckles. "I have an IUD. The only place your cum is going is to its grave."

He thrusts and bites my neck. "Don't say that. They'll hear you," he hisses. I roll my eyes. "I can't help it," he murmurs. "I have this sudden sick fascination with seeing you round and pregnant." I shudder. "Do you want kids, Addy?"

"This is a super weird conversation to have with your dick still in me," I murmur, deflecting. I do want kids, but the sudden panic at the way my body will change makes me want to puke. It's selfish and messed up, but again, I'm working on it. Swallowing, I ask a question I'd been thinking about earlier, mostly to change the subject. "Why didn't you just spank and fuck me in the other room? Why did you carry me in here?"

He leans up, which causes his hips to shift and his dick to slip out. We both groan, and his eyes drop to my spread thighs, where I'm sure I'm leaking our combined releases. His fingers find my pussy, and before I realize what he's doing, I feel him fingering me again. I shiver, too overstimulated to be pleased right now.

"Jack," I protest, trying to pull away.

He presses down on my back and tuts at me. "Just give me a minute." I shiver. "I brought you in here because the other room is a literal sub-space. It's a safe place for you or me to decompress and come back to our baseline. This is a playroom, and what I did to you didn't belong anywhere but in here." He finally pulls his fingers free with a satisfied grunt.

"What was that for?" I murmur, accepting his hand when he helps me up.

Grinning, he runs his cum coated fingers over my lips. "Open up, Addison."

I chuckle, unable to help myself from taunting him. "Just this once," I purr. "Only because you were such a good boy and fucked me so well."

Jack grunts, rolling his eyes. "You can't just shut up and do what you're told, can you?"

I wink and lick my lips. "Maybe you should fill my mouth up."

Growling, he shoves his fingers deep into my throat until I'm choking. My eyes gape, and he snickers. *Asshole.* "I was making sure my cum stayed where it belongs," he finally answers with a nonchalant shrug.

Holy shit.

The possessive, crazy bastard really is trying to knock me up. I fight a grin.

I love him.

Chapter Seventeen

THE FIRST THING I notice is the obvious feeling of someone staring at me. The second is the slight weight blanketing my body. My eyes blink open slowly. The room is dark, illuminated only by the electric fireplace on the opposite side of the couch. All of the candles have long since gone out. I hadn't meant for us to sleep in here all night. An ache forms in the pit of my stomach. Addy deserves a plush bed, not a couch. But before any negative feelings can settle in, my eyes lock on Addison's bright blue's as she greets me with her beautiful smiling face. My heart clenches painfully, and I suck in a sharp breath.

"Every morning," I whisper. She tilts her head to the side adorably. Her long blonde hair, that I spent a good hour detangling for her last night after fucking her again, spills over her naked chest. "I want to wake up like this every morning."

She swallows thickly before shaking it off with a giggle. "What, with my naked body on top of your hard dick?"

I groan, thrusting my hips up when I realize she's right. *Easy.* It would be so easy to slip inside of her. But not yet. Not until I make sure she understands. I shake my head and palm her neck, dragging her face to me. "No, Princess," I murmur, loving the way her eyes flare at the nickname. "With the love of my life in my arms."

She whimpers, but I smother the sound with my mouth. Kissing her now, in the light of day, with her happy, relaxed body covering mine, is more than I ever imagined I'd have in this life. With every ebb and flow of my lips, I try to tell her what I'm feeling. It's so much. More than should be possible.

Addison Hughes dug her way into my mind with one look six years ago. She engrained herself in my heart with one sassy comeback and glare. Then, she went and burrowed inside of me when she finally let her walls down last night. Now, she's in my bones–deep down to the very marrow...and she's never getting out. There are no bounds to what I'd give her–do for her.

We lose ourselves in each other, kissing languidly like we have all the time in the world. When we finally pull ourselves apart, we're panting heavily and looking at each other with glossy eyes. Leaning back and putting a few inches of space between us, she inhales a deep breath that has my body tensing and my heart pounding for a whole new reason.

"Jackson," she murmurs, licking her pink, swollen lips. Her gaze flicks to mine, and I immediately recognize the look there. She's open and vulnerable right now. Fully exposed, hiding nothing from me. It renders me speechless, so I just nod. "I have to apologize to you." I open my mouth to stop her, not liking the sound of that, but she presses her tiny finger to my lips, effectively silencing me. "No, please. Let me say this."

Brows furrowed, I drop down flat and wrap my arms around her body, sensing her anxiety. My hands begin slow, soothing tracks up and down her soft skin as I work to calm my heart. She just wants to talk. To apologize for some unknown reason. She's not leaving.

"Okay," I whisper. "I'm listening."

Smiling softly, she looks down at her hands that are bundled beneath her chin on my chest and begins to play with something there absently, but my eyes are locked on her. "I need to apologize for running all those months ago. And for everything I did before that." Swallowing, her eyes flutter closed. "I knew you had feelings for me from the beginning. I knew because I had them, too. Any time you walked in a room, anytime you looked at me, or fuck, smiled at me, I could feel it there, between us." She pauses, meeting my eyes. "It scared the shit out of me, Jack. It still does."

"Me too," I murmur, massaging her tight back muscles. "It scared me, too." She gives me a surprised look that has me grinning. "You're not the only one with monsters, Princess. I told you that."

"But it seems so easy for you," she cuts in, still partially shocked.

Tipping my shoulder the best I can on my back, I sigh. "You may have run, Addy, but I let you. You're not the only one who made a mistake." Reaching up, I run my fingers through her long hair, untangling the strands. My eyes lock on the flames of the fireplace as I think about how to word what I want to say. "Honestly, I think it was for the best. We ran hard, and we ran fast, but look how good it turned out when we finally crashed into each other." Looking back, I smile at her beautiful, sleepy face. "I think we were running toward one another the entire time. We just needed to make pitstops along the way to heal and figure shit out."

"And now?" she whispers.

I press my lips to her in a quick kiss. "And now, we run together."

Addison's breath wooshes against my face as she deflates happily. Her eyes lock onto mine as she slowly pulls one of her hands from under her chin and lifts it. My gaze snags on the small purple bracelet adorning her bruised wrist, and I'm suddenly torn on what to feel. On the one hand, I want to rage and shout about the bruises that are much darker today than last night. On the other, I want to bundle her up and spoil her for making me so happy.

She put it back on. Something so small and seemingly insignificant but means so much.

My fingers trail over the bruise softly as though I'm trying to erase it. Addy moves my thumb to the lilac metal cuff instead. "I am a broken, damaged woman full of monsters and chaos, but like a soothing balm, you're slowly healing my bruises." I swallow a sudden lump in my throat at her words. *Fuck*. That hit harder than anything else she could have said. "I love you, Jackson Lowell."

Except that.

Groaning, I slam my mouth into hers, devouring her lips and words with a ferocity that's probably painful for her, but I can't help it. My hands slide down her body, only pausing to palm her ass cheeks. I'm careful, knowing she's probably sore. I squeeze once, then grip her thighs and spread her legs wide for me. "Put me inside of you, Addison," I growl against her lips.

She moans at my words but sits up and does it. Her bare tits sway with her movements, and her hair drops to cover her eyes. I push it back, cupping her cheek as she slips me inside her wet, warm cunt. My head tips back, and a deep groan leaves my lips. "Oh my god," we both moan as she drops down fully.

Addy slowly lifts back up, rocking her hips at a slow, melodic pace. I find her eyes, and the love I see in them hits me dead in the chest. I tug her forward, causing her to land on me with a thud. She squeals, but the sound dies on her lips as I carefully flip us over, thankful that the couch is deep enough that it's practically a small bed. "Wrap your legs around me, Princess. I wanna feel all of you."

She does, banding her legs and arms around my body until every inch of her touches me. My forehead drops to hers as I roll my hips. "I love you, Addison," I breathe. Her walls tighten at the same time her arms do.

"Shit," she moans. "Say it again."

I smile against her neck, repeating the words again and again as I slowly make love to her. We spend hours getting lost in each other, declaring our love and promises as though we might die tomorrow. And who knows, maybe we will, but at least I'll go out knowing I've had the love of the greatest woman I've ever met.

"Fuck," she moans, her hips stuttering against me as I bring her to the brink of another orgasm. "Do it, Jackson. Fill me up, please. I need it."

She's been begging for my cum all morning. I think I might have created a little cum hungry demon with a breeding kink. "Shit," I groan, bouncing her on my cock from our spot on the fur rug in front of the fireplace. "Gonna knock you up someday, Addy. Mark my fucking words." I press my palm to her belly as though I can make her stupid IUD disappear with my touch alone. She shudders as she grips my thighs harder and leans back further to rub her clit across my pelvis. "Gonna put my baby right here."

That sends her over the edge just like I knew it would. She squeezes my cock so hard she forces me to follow. I bark out her name, thrusting in deep and holding her hips down on my cock, making sure nothing spills out. Fuck. I can't wait for the day when we're actually trying. Panting, she drops down on my chest with a giggle and peers up at me with sleepy, sated eyes.

I really need to feed her again. At one point, we stopped for a bowl of fruit left in the mini-fridge from last night, but it wasn't enough. I need to get her healthy again, and I can't do that if I keep fucking her through meals.

"Just think," I murmur once I've caught my breath. "One day, we'll be able to tell our kids that it all started at a kink party in a sex hotel on Valentine's Day."

She giggles, and the sound of it is like music to my ears. She cups my cheek and shakes her head. "No," she murmurs. "It started six years ago, the first time I looked at you."

♥ • ♥ • ♥ • ♥ • ♥

Two days later, we're checking out of the greatest hotel in existence. We're both exhausted, sated, and sore as fuck. But we're also in love and starting our future. I don't know what it looks like yet or what's in store for us. I know a lot of healing needs to happen for both of us. And I know real conversations need to be had when we're not lost in the lust and excitement of finally connecting after years of build-up. But I also know we'll handle it all together as a team.

"I can't wait to come back here," Addy sighs happily as the front desk attendant gathers our checkout paperwork. I look down at Addison, finding her eyes trailing over the parts of the hotel she missed the other night. Granted, the only reason I know what all is here is because I arrived hours before the event.

"You want to come back?" I ask, surprised but not unhappy about the idea. I loved playing with Addy in all ways, including everything that went down at the Valentine's party. Well, maybe not that fact that she could have denied me and left with someone else entirely, but the rest was hot as fuck.

She shoots me an incredulous look. "Of course I do." Shrugging, she tosses me an adorable grin. "I wouldn't mind trying out the tank," she says, referring to the glass voyeur box. My brows lift. "Maybe I'll even give the female glory hole a try." Okay...now she's just goading me. *I think.* I narrow my eyes at her, then melt when she falls into a fit of giggles. She's just so fucking cute.

The receptionist smiles widely, clearly overhearing our conversation. She passes us our receipts and then reaches over the desk and picks up a flyer. "Here," she says, passing it to Addison and me. "If you really want to join us again and try something new, we're having a Swingers Party in May. Full use of the rooms is permitted with couples who find a partner, pair, or more, to play with."

Swinging?

I look down at Addy, once again surprised when she shrugs and grins widely at me. Tugging me by the sleeve, she brings me down to whisper in my ear. "It might be fun to play with another man. Have a repeat of the other night." I swallow thickly. "I think I'd like to watch you dominate and fuck a hot guy," she purrs before adding, "*or two.*"

The End...For Now.

That was...

Wow.

That was....

Delicious, in my humble opinion.

Steamy af if you ask my panties.

Either way, I hope you enjoyed the beginning of Jack and Addy's story as much as I did.

If you couldn't tell from the way it left off, there's way more where this came from.

Jack and Addy meet a certain red-headed brother and his partner at a certain party and well, things take off from there.

Jack, Addy, Stephen and Dom—your new fav poly family.

It's a journey. A learning experience. And a beautiful new beginning, for all of them.

Catch their story in the next installment of Carnal Expectations,

Dominate Me.

Coming soon to KU.

Also By

Author Bex Dawn

The Los Diablos world encompasses these three series (for now!)
For full reading order, please visit my website.
They are all still growing, but these are the books you can read/preorder now!

Los Diablos Syndicate

Crash(Prequel)

Burn

Evolve

Resurrect

Prevail

The Trichotomy of New York

Violet Craves (Prequel)

Rough Love

Tough Love

Sons Of Satan MC
Brass-Part One
Chains

This series is a separate world. These are stand-alone, loosely interwoven, that take place in the town of Blue River, Colorado.
They each follow a different couple, and their very specific kinks!

Carnal Expectations
Cracked Foundation
Primal Urges
Santa's Baby
Power Struggle
Dominate Me

About Author

Bex Dawn

Hey there Smut Sluts! Welcome to my world. My name is Bex, and I am a 30-something bibliophile from California. I own a beauty salon, five rescue animals, and a shit ton of books. I have been writing since I could hold a pencil. My mom used to love to tell stories about the "books" I would write as a child. I would apparently scribble nonsense on paper and then proceed to "read" my books to everyone who would listen. Not much has changed since other than the fact that I've changed out the pencil and paper for a fancy laptop.

Writing and creative arts have always held a place close to my heart, but it wasn't until an extremely dark time in my life recently that I really pushed myself to fulfill my lifelong dream of publishing.

In the darkest days of my life, books saved me. Other people's written words dragged me out of my depression, kicking and screaming. And for that, I will forever be grateful. My dream is that my words will have a similar impact on even one person out there.

So, here's to sexy, possessive, alpha holes and kinky fuckery!

Follow me on social media!

www.authorbexdawn.com

TikTok: @bexdawnwrites

Instagram: @bexdawnwrites

Amazon: Bex Dawn

Facebook Reader Group: Author Bex Dawn

Interested in ARC reading for Bex Dawn? We're always looking to add to our team

Printed in Great Britain
by Amazon

40015343R00096